THE BEGINNING . . .

"You cannot do this!" Susannah Goode shrieked, fear choking her throat. "You cannot do this to us!"

The officers roughly dragged Susannah and her mother to the door. She heard surprised murmurs as they passed through the commons. Whispered questions.

The prison loomed ahead, a low clapboard building behind the meetinghouse.

"Why are you doing this to us?" Susannah cried, the words bursting from her throat. "Why are you dragging us from our home?"

Benjamin Fier stopped on the path. His voice was low and steady. His eyes locked onto Susannah's.

"You two will burn before the week is out," he said.

Books by R. L. Stine

Available from ARCHWAY Paperbacks

THE FEAR STREET® SAGA ①

R·L·STINE

The
Betrayal

AN ARCHWAY PAPERBACK
Published by POCKET BOOKS
New York   London   Toronto   Sydney   Tokyo   Singapore

AN ARCHWAY PAPERBACK *Original*

An Archway Paperback published by
POCKET BOOKS, a division of Simon & Schuster Inc.
1230 Avenue of the Americas, New York, NY 10020

Copyright © 1993 by Parachute Press, Inc.

ISBN: 0-671-86831-4

First Archway Paperback printing August 1993

18 17 16 15 14 13 12 11 10

FEAR STREET is a registered trademark of
Parachute Press, Inc.

AN ARCHWAY PAPERBACK and colophon are
registered trademarks of Simon & Schuster Inc.

Cover art by Bill Schmidt

Printed in the U.S.A.

IL 7+

THE FIER FAMILY TREE

Constance=Matthew (brothers) Benjamin=Margaret
(b. 1675) (b. 1660)   (b. 1653) (b. 1657)

        Mary   Edward=Rebecca
      (b. 1693)   (b. 1674) (b. 1686)

                                    Ezra
                                 (b. 1704)

The
Betrayal

Village of Shadyside
1900

The fire roared like thunder. Above the choking clouds of black smoke, the night sky brightened with a wash of angry scarlet.

The flames tossed and crashed like ocean waves, rolling over the blackened mansion, pouring out every window, sweeping up the walls and over the roof until the house was nothing more than the dark core of a raging fireball.

Staring down at the fire from the low hill that overlooked the wide lawn, Nora Goode pressed her hands over her ears. But even with the fire's roar muffled she could hear the screams.

The screams of those trapped inside the blazing Fear mansion.

The screams of everyone she knew, of everyone she loved.

"Daniel! Come out!" Nora cried, her small voice buried under the avalanche of terrified shrieks, anguished moans, and the unending roar of the spreading flames.

"Daniel, I'm here! I am alive! I ran out! I escaped the fire!" Nora shouted. "Where are you? Are you coming out too?"

The flames roared louder, as if to answer her.

Nora's entire body trembled in dread.

She lowered one hand to the amulet on a chain around her neck.

The fire had already blazed for more than an hour. Daniel wasn't coming out. No one was coming out.

Only minutes after the fire had begun, the Shadyside volunteer fire fighters had pulled their horse-drawn water truck onto the lawn of the mansion. But the flames had already swallowed up the entire house.

Their faces revealing horror and awe, the fire fighters stood by helplessly and watched with the other townspeople who had gathered on the low hill, huddling in small groups, their faces red in the light of the flickering blaze.

"You're not coming out, are you, Daniel?" Nora said. "I'll never see you again."

She shut her eyes. But even with her eyes closed she could still see the angry red and orange flames tossing across the inside of her eyelids.

Squeezing the small round pendant tightly, Nora sighed. This silver amulet with its sparkling blue jewels held in place by a silver three-toed claw, like those on a tiny bird's foot, had been given to her by Daniel Fear as a token of his love.

"It is all I have left of you, Daniel!" Nora wailed.

Voices rose around her, close by, louder than the thunder of the flames. Nora opened her eyes and turned her gaze on the horrified faces of the people from the village. They clung together, as if frightened for their own lives.

"The fire will burn forever!" a bearded man cried, his face scarlet, the flames reflected in his eyes.

"Look at the house," a frail woman a few feet from Nora cried, pointing. "It is covered with flames, but it does not burn!"

"It looks as if the *sky* is on fire!" screamed a little girl, hiding her face in her mother's dark skirt.

"I always knew this place was evil," the bearded man declared, shielding his eyes with one hand. "I always knew the Fears would come to no good."

"They burned up inside their house," someone said.

"May their evil perish with them," another person added.

"The firemen did not even try to put it out."

"They could not put out *this* fire. It is not an ordinary fire. It is not a fire from this world."

"The evil of this house feeds the fire."

"The house is cursed! The ground is cursed!"

"No! Please . . . stop it! *Stop it!*" Nora shrieked.

Unable to shut out their voices, she began running toward the house. Her cloak flapped behind her as she stumbled down the hill and over the lawn.

Slipping on the dew-wet grass, she could feel the heat of the fire on her face. Strange shadows flickered over the lawn, black against the reflected scarlet light.

"Daniel, why is your family so cursed?" Nora cried as she ran. "What kind of evil brought you and your family to this fiery end?"

Nora's long dark hair floated wildly above the flapping cloak. As she ran, she held her arms out as if ready to embrace the flames.

"Who *is* that?"

"Where is she going?"

"Somebody stop her!"

Alarmed voices rang out from the crowd.

Panting loudly, Nora raised an arm to shield her eyes as she ran. She could feel the precious silver amulet bobbing against her throat.

"Daniel, are you in there? Daniel?"

"Somebody stop her!"

"Has she gone mad?"

"Who *is* she? Is she a Fear?"

The voices finally faded, drowned out by the crackle and roar of the blinding red-orange blaze.

It's so hot, so hot! Nora thought. She loosened the cloak and let it fall.

I feel as if I am running into the sun! Now I feel as if I am on fire too.

She stopped, choking on the hot smoke.

Where am I?

She gazed into the flames and suddenly realized she was standing in front of a window. The window of the grand ballroom.

The tossing flames made the window glow.

"Ohhh!" Nora moaned in horror as the faces inside came into view. Faces among the flames.

Nora's breath caught in her throat as she stared through the window at the wriggling dark bodies.

Are they dancing in there? Dancing with the flames? No.

Their faces were twisted in agony. Their dark bodies writhing in pain.

She saw screaming women, flames rolling up from their hair.

She saw the tortured faces of young men, dark holes where their eyes should have been, their clothing wrapped in fire.

Who *are* these people? Nora wondered, unable to turn her eyes from the ghastly nightmare inside the house. Why are they in the ballroom? Why aren't they consumed by the flames?

Why don't they *die?*

And then Nora's eyes focused on a figure in the center of the writhing, screaming crowd. A young girl. Wearing a long maroon dress and an old-fashioned cap.

Nora gasped as the girl raised her head and their eyes met.

The girl's eyes were eggshell white. Glowing white.

As Nora gaped in horror, she saw the girl's mouth open wide into a tortured scream, a scream of rage, of unbearable pain.

Then Nora noticed that the girl's hands were tied behind her. Tied to a tall wooden pole.

The girl was tied to a stake.

And now her dress was billowing with fire. And the flames were rising up to her face, up to her long blond hair. The cap burst into flame then.

Struggling against the stake, the girl shrieked as she burned.

Then, with a low explosion, the flames hid them all behind a rippling yellow curtain.

The window burst, glass shattering and flying out. The fire's roar rumbled over her.

And still Nora stood motionless, staring where the screaming girl had been, staring into the wall of flame, staring, staring into the bright, dancing horror. . . .

PART ONE

Wickham Village, Massachusetts Colony
1692

Chapter
1

The fire crackled softly. A loud pop sent up a shower of glowing red embers.

Susannah Goode uttered a cry of surprise and jumped back from the hearth. The embers died at her feet.

After straightening the starched white apron she wore over her heavy, dark maroon skirt, Susannah bent over the bake kettle to lift the heavy lid and peer inside.

Behind her in the small borning room, the baby started to cry. Susannah heard the floorboards creak as her mother made her way to the cradle to see what the problem was.

"Susannah!" Martha Goode's tone was scolding. "You have wrapped George too tightly again. The poor baby can barely breathe!"

"The blanket is too small. I had trouble covering him," Susannah complained, still bent over the kettle, a few long golden curls falling out of her bun and over her face.

"The blanket will have to do," her mother replied. "It is the best we can afford." She lifted the squalling baby and held him up to her face. "Poor George. Poor George. What did your sister do to you?"

Susannah sighed. "These biscuits are taking so long to bake."

Martha Goode stepped up behind her. George's cries had softened to quiet whimpers as he lay his head against his mother's stiff white collar.

"The fire is too low," her mother said, shaking her head disapprovingly. "You cannot bake in those dying embers. Put more wood on, Susannah."

Frowning, Susannah straightened up and tossed the locks of escaped hair behind the white collar that covered the shoulders of her dress. "We need firewood."

Susannah was tall and thin. She had sparkling blue eyes, creamy pale skin, and dimples in both cheeks when she smiled.

Whenever Martha Goode found Susannah gazing into the looking glass or toying with her golden hair, she scolded her with the same words: "True beauty comes from deeds, not appearance, Daughter."

As a Puritan, Susannah had been endlessly taught the virtue of modesty. She had been taught that all righteous people are beautiful and the same in the eyes of the Maker.

She felt embarrassed whenever her mother caught her admiring herself, as if her mother had peered inside her soul and found it flawed and unworthy.

But at sixteen, Susannah felt stirrings that excited her as much as they troubled her. She found herself thinking of a certain boy, daydreaming about him as she worked. And she couldn't help but wonder if she was pretty enough to win him over all the other girls in the village of Wickham.

Martha Goode held the baby and rocked him gently as she stared disapprovingly at the fire. "Where is your father? He will want his biscuits on time, but he will not have them if he is not here."

"I believe he is at the commons, tending the cows," Susannah told her.

"Cows," her mother scoffed. "Bags of bone, you mean." She lowered her gaze sadly to the baby she held. "It is a wonder we survive, George."

Susannah started toward the door. "I will get the firewood and fetch Father. I was going out for a walk anyway," Susannah insisted.

"Susannah. Please," her mother said, fear clouding her eyes. "You must stop taking solitary walks. You must not do anything—anything at all—to attract attention to yourself."

She gazed intently at her pretty daughter. Then she added in a low whisper, "You know the dangers. You know what is going on here."

"Yes, Mother," Susannah replied impatiently. "But I think I can go out for a walk without—"

"They took Abigail Hopping from her house last

night and dragged her to the prison," her mother said softly. "The poor woman's screams woke me."

Susannah uttered a shocked gasp. "Abigail Hopping a *witch?*"

"That's what Benjamin Fier says," Martha Goode replied, swallowing hard. "Benjamin accused Abigail of singing songs of the Evil One as she prepared the evening meal."

"I cannot believe that Abigail Hopping is a witch," Susannah said, shaking her head. "Has she confessed?"

"Her trial is at the meetinghouse tonight," Martha Goode said darkly.

"Oh, Mother! Will she burn like the others?" Susannah cried, choking out the words.

Her mother rocked the baby and didn't reply. "There is so much evil about, Daughter," she said finally. "Three witches uncovered in our village by Benjamin Fier since summer began. I beg you to be careful, Susannah. Stay in the shadows. Give no one reason to suspect you—or even to notice you."

Susannah nodded. "Yes, Mother. I am only going to the commons for firewood. I shall be back quickly." She pushed open the door, causing a flood of bright sunlight to wash over the dark room.

"No! Stop!" her mother cried.

Halfway out the door Susannah turned, her blue eyes flashing, an impatient frown on her face.

"Are you going out with your head uncovered?" Martha Goode demanded. "Where are your thoughts, dear?"

"I am sorry." Susannah returned to the room, took

her white cap from its peg, and pulled it down over her hair. "I will hurry back," she said.

She closed the door behind her and, shielding her eyes with one hand from the bright afternoon sunlight, made her way past the chickens pecking the dirt in front of the house.

Susannah turned onto the path that led into the village. Walking quickly, her long skirt trailing over the dirt, she passed the Halseys' house. The glass for their windows hadn't yet arrived from England, Susannah saw. The windows were boarded up. Mr. Halsey was bent over his vegetable garden and didn't look up.

At the meetinghouse she saw someone up on the shingle roof working to attach a brass weather vane above the chimney.

The village magistrate, Benjamin Fier, a troubled expression on his face, was just entering the building. Susannah stopped short and waited until he had disappeared inside. A cold shudder ran down her back as she thought of Abigail Hopping.

I know Benjamin Fier is a good and righteous man, Susannah thought. But I am afraid of him, just as everyone else in Wickham is.

As village magistrate, Benjamin Fier was the most powerful man in Wickham. He was also the wealthiest.

His home, the biggest in the village, stood across from the meetinghouse. The aroma of roasting beef wafted out from the summer kitchen as Susannah strode past.

The Fiers are so prosperous, Susannah thought,

unable to suppress a feeling of envy. They won't be having biscuits and gravy for their dinner. The Fiers can have roasted meat every night.

Susannah knew that the Fier brothers, Benjamin and Matthew, were the most prosperous men in Wickham because they were the most worthy. Since she had been a little girl, she'd been taught that good fortune goes to those who are the most righteous.

Thus, Benjamin Fier became magistrate because he was the wisest, most pious man in the village. It was he who conducted the witchcraft trials. And he who insisted the guilty ones be burned—rather than hanged as they were elsewhere in Massachusetts. Benjamin's younger brother Matthew had a farm that prospered when others failed because Matthew Fier was more righteous and faithful than the other farmers.

That was plain and simple knowledge.

As she passed the meetinghouse and glanced toward the commons, Susannah found herself thinking about Benjamin's son, Edward Fier.

Edward, where are you?

Are you thinking about me?

"Oh!" she cried as she stumbled over an enormous pink pig spotted with black, and went sprawling onto the hard ground.

The pig grunted a loud protest and scrambled off the path.

Susannah picked herself up and brushed the dust off the front of her white apron. That will teach me not to have improper thoughts, she scolded herself, straightening her cap over her hair.

But how can thoughts about Edward be improper?

She saw her father at the far end of the commons, the large, rectangular pasture in the center of the village. He was busily raking a section of ground and didn't see Susannah wave to him.

Mr. Franklin, the blacksmith, was at his anvil in front of his shop, pounding noisily on a sheet of tin as Susannah hurried past. She smiled at Franklin's apprentice, a boy named Arthur Kent, who was tending the bellows, which were nearly twice as big as he was.

Behind the blacksmith's shop were the shimmering green woods. Tall poplars and beech trees leaned in toward the village. Behind these the woods grew dark with pines, oaks, and maples.

A village woodpile stood at the edge of the woods, logs neatly chopped and stacked. But Susannah's eyes were focused on the woods.

Sunlight filtered down through the shimmering leaves, sending rays of light darting over the ground. Black and gold monarch butterflies fluttered in and out of the shafts of white light.

I shall take a short walk into the woods, Susannah decided.

It felt good to be out of the dark house, away from the heat of the cooking hearth, away from the crying baby.

Away from her chores and the watchful eyes of her mother.

Away from the heavy fear that hovered over the entire village these days.

Susannah stepped into the woods, dry twigs cracking beneath her heavy black shoes. As soon as she was hidden by the trees, she pulled off her cap and shook her hair free.

She walked slowly, raising her face to the shafts of bright sunlight. Her dress caught on a low bramble. She tugged it free and kept walking.

A scrabbling sound nearby made her spin around, just in time to see a brown and white chipmunk scurry under a pile of dead leaves.

Susannah tossed her long hair back and took a deep breath. The air smelled piney and sweet.

I'm not supposed to enjoy the woods, she thought, her smile slowly fading. Susannah had been taught that the woods were a place of evil.

As if mirroring her thoughts, the trees grew thicker, shutting out the sunlight. It became evening-dark.

Away from civilization, deep in the woods, was where the Evil One and his followers dwelt, Susannah had been taught.

The witches of the village came here to dance their evil dances by moonlight with the Evil One and his servants. The Evil One and his servants lived deep in holes in the ground, hidden by scrub and thick shrubs. Susannah believed that if she wandered alone into the darkness of their domain, they might reach up and grab her and pull her down, down into their netherworld of eternal torture and darkness.

The air grew cooler. From a low branch just above Susannah's head a dove uttered a deep-throated moan, cold and sorrowful.

Susannah shuddered.

"It is so dark, suddenly so cold," she said.

Time to go back.

As she turned, she felt strong hands grab her from behind.

"The Evil One!" she cried.

Chapter
2

"Let go of me!" Susannah screamed.

To her surprise, the hands obediently released her. She spun around, her blue eyes wide with fright, and stared into the laughing face of Edward Fier. "Do I look like the Evil One to you?" he asked.

Susannah felt her face redden. She glared angrily at him. "Yes, you must be the Evil One," she said. "Why else would you be out in these woods?"

"I followed you," he replied, his expression solemn.

Edward was tall and good-looking. He wore a wide-brimmed black hat over his straight dark brown hair, which fell below his ears. His gray doublet was made of the finest linen. The cuffs at the end of his sleeves were white and stiffly starched.

His navy blue breeches ended just below the knee.

Gray wool stockings covered his legs. On his feet were Dutch-style clogs fashioned of dark leather.

No other young man in the village dressed as well as Edward. He seemed to take his clothing as seriously as he did everything else in life. In private some villagers criticized his fancy dress, accusing him of the sin of pride.

But no one dared criticize him in public. For Edward was a Fier, Benjamin Fier's son. And no one would dare say a word against Magistrate Fier or his son.

As the trees shuddered around them in a sudden cold breeze, Edward's dark brown eyes locked on Susannah's. "We should not joke about the Evil One," he said, lowering his voice. "My father says the Evil One's slaves have overrun our village."

"I—I am so afraid these days," Susannah confessed, lowering her gaze to the dark ground. "I keep dreaming about Faith Warburton. She—she was my friend," Susannah stammered.

"I know," Edward muttered softly.

"They seized her as a witch . . . because she wore a red ribbon in her hair. Th-they *burned* her—!" Susannah's words were cut short by a sob.

Edward placed a hand on Susannah's trembling shoulder. "I know that my father must have had proof of your friend's evil practices. He appears stern, but he is a fair and just man, Susannah."

"We should not be here together. We have to stop our secret meetings. They put me in great danger," Susannah said softly.

"You are in no danger," Edward replied. "I . . . wanted to talk to you, Susannah. I wanted to—"

Before Susannah could back away, Edward had his arms around her waist. He lowered his face to hers and kissed her.

The hat tumbled off his head, and he pressed his lips against hers, urgently, hungrily.

Susannah was breathless when she finally pulled free. "You—you are suffocating me!" she exclaimed, grinning at him. She raised a hand to his shoulder. "What if the Evil One is watching us?" she teased.

To her surprise, he pulled away from her touch. His dark eyes flared with anger. "I *told* you," he warned, "do not joke about the Evil One."

"But, Edward—" she began. His intensity always startled her.

"You know I cannot bear blasphemy," he interrupted in a low, steady voice.

They had been meeting secretly for weeks, stealing moments behind the grain barn or behind the trees at the riverbank. Susannah had been surprised by Edward's seriousness, by his solemn attitude about most things.

She liked to tease but quickly learned he didn't share her sense of humor.

Why did she care so much about him? Why did she think about him night and day? Why did she dream about being with him forever?

Because he needed her. Because he seemed to feel as she did.

She gazed up at him coyly. "Being here alone together in the woods, that is a crime against village custom," she said. "What do you think your father would say?"

He picked up his hat from the ground, gripping it tightly in one hand. "Being here with you, Susannah, is no crime."

"Why is that?" she teased.

He hesitated, gazing at her as if trying to see inside her head, to read her thoughts. "Because we love each other," he said finally.

And before she knew it, they were wrapped in each other's arms again.

I want to stay here, Susannah thought happily. Stay here with Edward in the dark woods. Live in the wild together, just the two of us, away from the village, away from everyone.

She pressed her cheek against his, surprised that his face was as hot as hers.

A sudden noise made her cry out and pull away.

Voices!

"Edward—someone else is here!" she cried, raising her hands to her cheeks in horror. "We're caught!"

Chapter

3

Edward's dark eyes grew wide with fear. He grasped Susannah's hand tightly.

They listened, frozen together in the dark woods as if they'd been turned to stone.

The voices rose, carried by the wind.

Chanting voices.

"Burn the witch! Burn the witch! Burn the witch!"

"Ohhh!" Susannah gasped.

The chanting voices weren't coming from nearby. The wind was carrying the sound from the commons.

"There is no one here," Edward said, smiling with relief.

"Poor Abigail Hopping," Susannah whispered.

"If she is a witch, she must face the fire," Edward replied, still holding Susannah's hand.

Susannah rested her head against his shoulder. "We should get back. I went out for firewood. I should have been home. My mother will think the Evil One has taken me."

"You go first," he told her. "I will wait here a while before I return."

"Are you going to tell your father . . . about us?" Susannah asked eagerly.

"Yes," Edward told her. "When the time is right."

She leaned forward and kissed him again. She didn't want to leave. She didn't want to go back to her tiny, dark house. She didn't want to return to all the anger and fear of the village.

Edward gave her a gentle push, his hands on her shoulders. "Go."

She forced a smile, then turned and ran off, pulling on the cap and covering her hair.

We're going to be married, she thought, her heart pounding.

Edward and I are going to be married.

I am going to be the wife of Edward Fier.

She felt as if she were floating through the trees.

Susannah ran right past the woodpile and through the commons, and was nearly home before she remembered she had come out for firewood, and had to go back.

"The carrots are small but sweet," William Goode said. He sat stiffly at the head of the table, rubbing gravy off the wooden plate with a biscuit.

Susannah watched her father eat his dinner. He

looked tired to her, tired and old. He was not yet forty, yet his face was lined, and his once-blond hair had turned prematurely white.

"Susannah baked the biscuits," Martha Goode said.

"Would you like more gravy, Father?" Susannah asked, gesturing to the gravy pot still simmering on the hearth. "There are more boiled carrots, too."

"I am going to mash some carrots and give them to George when he wakes up," Susannah's mother said.

"I do not know why our carrots are so small," Mr. Goode grumbled. "Matthew Fier's carrots are as long as candles."

"Why do you not ask him his secret?" Susannah's mother suggested.

William Goode scowled. He narrowed his gray-green eyes at his wife. "Matthew Fier has no farming skills that I do not have. He has no secrets that I—"

"The Fiers have plenty of secrets," his wife interrupted. "Who *are* they, these Fier brothers? Where do they come from? They did not come to the New World from England, as we did."

"I do not know," Mr. Goode replied thoughtfully. "They come from a small farm village. That is all I know. They were poor when they arrived, both Fier brothers and their wives. But they have prospered here. And that proves they are pious folk, favored by the Maker."

His wife sighed. "These carrots are sweet enough, William. I did not intend to hurt your feelings."

William Goode frowned. "Sweet enough," he muttered.

"Help me clear the dinner table, Susannah," Martha Goode ordered. "Why are you sitting there with that dazed, faraway expression on your face?"

"Sorry, Mother." Susannah started to get up, but her father placed a hand on her arm to restrain her.

"Susannah will clear the table in a little while," he told his wife. "I wish to speak with her first." He stood up, pulled a clay pipe down from his pipe rack, filled it with tobacco from his cloth pouch, and went over to the fire to light it.

Susannah turned in her chair, her eyes trained on her father, trying to read his expression. "What did you wish to speak to me about, Father?"

"About Edward Fier," he replied, frowning as he puffed hard to start the tobacco burning.

Susannah gasped. She had never discussed Edward with either of her parents. She and Edward were merely acquaintances, as far as her parents knew.

Holding the long white pipe by the bowl, Mr. Goode made his way back to the dinner table. He pulled back the stool next to Susannah's and sat down stiffly.

"Wh-what about him?" Susannah stammered, clasping her hands tightly in her lap.

Her father leaned close to her. Pipe smoke rose up in front of him, encircling them both in a fragrant cloud. "You and Edward Fier have been seen walking together," he accused. "Walking together without a chaperon present."

Susannah's mouth dropped open. She took a deep breath, then started to speak, but no sound came out.

"Do you deny it, Daughter?" Her father's white

eyebrows arched over his gray-green eyes, which burned accusations into hers. "Do you deny it?"

"No, Father," Susannah replied softly.

"You were seen in the woods together," her father continued sternly. He held the pipe close to his face but didn't smoke it.

"Yes, Father," Susannah muttered, her heart thudding in her chest. Then the words just burst out of her. She had been longing to tell her parents. Now she could hold back the news no longer.

"Edward and I are in love!" she cried. "He wants to marry me! Is that not wonderful?"

Her mother turned from the hearth, her eyes wide with surprise.

William Goode's face reddened. He lowered his pipe to the table. "Daughter, have you lost your senses? Are you living in a world of dreams?"

Susannah gaped at him. "Didn't you *hear* me, Father? Edward wants to marry me!"

Her father shut his eyes. He cleared his throat loudly. The pipe trembled in his hand. "You cannot marry Edward Fier," he said quietly.

"What are you saying?" Susannah whispered. "Why can't I?"

"Because Edward Fier is already betrothed," Mr. Goode replied flatly.

Susannah gasped. "What?"

"Edward Fier is engaged to be married," her father said. "Edward is to marry a young woman of Portsmouth. His father told me this morning."

Chapter
4

The hearth fire flickered low. Long shadows slipped across the floor. In her sleeping alcove, huddled under an old feather quilt, Susannah turned her face to the wall.

How could Edward be so cruel? she asked herself for the thousandth time.

How could he lead me to believe that he cared for me, that he *loved* me?

Susannah pressed her face into the pillow to muffle her sobs.

She had gone to bed early, hoping her parents wouldn't see how upset she was. Hours had passed now. A pale half moon was high in the late night sky, and Susannah was still wide awake, still tossing in her narrow bed, crying softly and thinking about Edward with anger and disbelief.

I trusted Edward, she thought. I believed everything he said. I risked my reputation for him.

And all the while he was engaged to another girl.

Breathing hard, Susannah rolled over and stared at the glowing embers in the fireplace across the room. Her secret meetings with Edward Fier rolled through her mind. She remembered his words, his touch, his kisses.

Edward always seemed trustworthy, she thought miserably. So honest and upright.

So good.

Susannah kicked off the quilt and pushed at the pillow, punching it with both hands.

I will never trust anyone again, she told herself bitterly. *Never!*

Across the commons, firelight blazed in the windows of Benjamin Fier's two-story house. In the dining room Benjamin was standing at one end of the oak table, gripping the back of a hand-carved chair.

Benjamin's son Edward glared at him defiantly from the other end of the table.

Benjamin was big and broad-shouldered, an imposing man who looked as if he could wrestle a bull and win. He had straight black hair that fell below his ears and bushy black eyebrows over small dark eyes that seemed to be able to pierce through anything.

Benjamin's face was red and almost always set in a hard frown. He was so powerful in appearance, his expression so angry, that most people in Wickham were afraid of him, which didn't displease him in the least.

Standing with his back to the fire, Benjamin unfastened the long row of brass buttons down the front of his black doublet, his dark eyes studying Edward.

"I will not obey you, Father," Edward insisted, his voice trembling. He had never defied his father. He knew it was wrong.

Benjamin stared across the table, his features set. He didn't reply.

"I cannot obey you, Father," Edward said when his father did not reply. "I will not marry Anne Ward." Edward gripped the back of the chair. He hoped his father could not see his trembling knees.

"You will marry the girl in the autumn," Benjamin said in his deep baritone. "I have arranged the marriage with her father."

He turned away from Edward to indicate that the discussion had ended. Picking up a poker, he jabbed at the logs in the fireplace, sending a shower of sparks flying up the brick chimney.

Edward swallowed hard.

Can I do this? he asked himself. Can I stand up to my father? Am I strong enough?

Another question nagged at Edward as he struggled to find words: Is it *right* to argue with my father? Is it not my duty to obey his wishes?

No! Edward answered his own question. I love Susannah Goode. I will marry Susannah and no one else. I *cannot* obey my father's wishes this time. I will not!

Edward took a deep breath. "Sir," he called, causing Benjamin to turn away from the fire. "I cannot marry Anne Ward. I do not know her. She is a stranger."

"You will become acquainted with her after the wedding," Benjamin said sternly. "It is a very fortunate arrangement for us."

"It is not fortunate for *me!*" Edward declared heatedly.

"Do not raise your voice to me, Edward," Benjamin warned, his face a dark crimson. He raised the fireplace poker and pointed it at his son. "Anne Ward is an excellent match for you."

"But I do not know her, Father! I do not love her!" Edward cried shrilly.

"Love?" Benjamin tossed back his head and laughed. "Edward, we did not come to these colonies for love. My brother, Matthew, and I did not leave our village for love. We came here to succeed! We came here to escape the poverty of our lives, to escape it *forever!*"

"I know, Father," Edward said, sighing. "But—"

"Do you know how poor our family was in the Old Country?" Benjamin demanded, setting down the heavy iron poker and returning to the table. His eyes burned into Edward's, hotter than the fireplace flames.

"Do you know how poor Matthew and I were? We ate *rats* to survive, Edward!"

"I know, sir—" Edward tried to interrupt. He had heard this speech before.

"Many was the night we huddled together to keep warm," Benjamin continued. "We had no fire, no blankets . . ."

Edward lowered his gaze to the floor. He held his breath, waiting for his chance to speak.

"We came to the New World to succeed, Edward. Not just to succeed but to prosper."

"You have done well, sir," Edward broke in. "You are the respected magistrate of Wickham. And Uncle Matthew's farm is the most—"

"We can do better!" Benjamin exploded, slamming his fist on the tabletop. "Your marriage to Anne Ward will help us do better, Edward."

"Why, Father? I don't see—"

"August Ward is the tea importer for Portsmouth," Benjamin explained, lowering his voice. "It has made him a very wealthy man. As his son-in-law, you will become a tea importer too. You will share his wealth."

"No, Father." Edward shook his head. "I cannot. I will not."

"You will," his father insisted sternly. "You must. You must marry August Ward's daughter."

"I cannot, Father! I am in love with someone else!" The words burst out of Edward's mouth before he could stop them. He gasped, realizing what he had revealed.

For a brief moment Benjamin's eyes widened with surprise. Then his expression quickly darkened. "In love?" he asked, his voice rising sarcastically. "With whom?" He made his way down the long table to confront his son. "With whom?" he demanded again, bringing his face a few inches from Edward's.

"Susannah Goode," Edward replied weakly. He cleared his throat and tried to avoid his father's harsh stare.

Benjamin hesitated, stunned. Then he closed his eyes and began to laugh—scornful laughter.

"D-do not laugh, sir," Edward stammered. "I am in love with Susannah Goode, and I wish to marry her."

Benjamin Fier shook his head, his smile lingering. "William Goode owns two scrawny chickens and two cows. His daughter is not a match for you, my son."

Edward took a deep breath, trying to calm his pounding heart. In his seventeen years he had never argued with his father, never dared to disagree with him.

Please, he prayed silently, *give me the strength to stand up to my father now. I know I am right. I know I cannot betray Susannah. Please give me the strength.*

"Sir," Edward began, "Susannah is a pious girl. She is the girl I will marry. I cannot marry a girl for her wealth. I must marry for love."

Benjamin closed his eyes. A log cracked loudly in the fireplace. The floorboards creaked as Benjamin shifted his weight. He sighed wearily. "Your engagement to Anne Ward is arranged. We will travel to Portsmouth in the autumn for your wedding. I wish your mother, Margaret, bless her soul, were alive to see you wed so profitably."

"No!" Edward cried. "No, Father!" He could feel his anger rise, feel the heat of it in his chest, feel himself losing control—for the first time in his life. "I have always obeyed you, sir. I know you are a wise and honorable man. But it is *my* life!" Edward screamed, his hands balled into tight fists at his waist. "It is my life, and I will marry Susannah Goode! I will marry her even if we have to run away to do it!"

Edward turned from his father and ran from the room.

I did it, he thought, relief mixing with his anger as he made his way to his bedroom. I said what I had to say. I stood up to my father.

Back in the narrow dining room Benjamin Fier slumped heavily into a chair. He fingered the shiny buttons of his doublet as he stared thoughtfully into the fire.

Before long, a dark smile spread over the man's ruddy face. "I am sorry, Edward, my poor, confused son," he said, grinning into the leaping flames. "You will never marry Susannah Goode."

Chapter
5

"I dislike peeling potatoes!" Susannah groaned.

Her mother, seated in front of the hearth with the baby on her lap, raised her eyes to Susannah, her features tight with concern. "Are you feeling well, Daughter? It isn't your nature to complain."

"I am feeling well," Susannah replied, sighing.

I shall never feel well again, she thought miserably. Never, never, never.

She wanted to tell her mother everything, tell her about Edward and how he had lied to her, how he had betrayed her.

But Susannah knew she had to keep her broken heart a secret. Her meetings with Edward were against all rules of conduct.

Susannah had sinned, and now she was paying for

her sins. Paying with an empty feeling that gnawed at her without relief, paying with a heavy sadness she knew she'd never shake.

Martha Goode rose from her chair, cradling the sleeping baby in one arm, and stepped up behind Susannah at the table. She put her free hand to Susannah's forehead. "Hmmm. You feel a little warm, Daughter. Do you feel feverish?"

Susannah lowered her knife and gazed up at her mother. "I am not ill," she said impatiently. "I just detest peeling potatoes. They are so wet and slippery."

Martha Goode took a step back, startled by Susannah's vehemence. "We should all be thankful that we have been given potatoes for our meal," she said softly. "Your father works so hard, Susannah. It is a sin to complain if there is food on the table."

"Yes, Mother," Susannah relented, lowering her eyes.

Edward's face flashed into her mind. His thick brown hair. His dark eyes.

Where are you now, Edward? Susannah wondered, picking up another potato to peel. What are you doing?

I know you are not thinking about me.

Are you thinking about your bride? Are you packing your bags? Preparing for your journey to Portsmouth?

She uttered a long sigh and stabbed the knife blade into the potato.

"Susannah, are you sure you are not ill?" her mother demanded.

"No. Not ill," Susannah muttered, unable to shake Edward from her mind.

"The potatoes can wait," her mother said, returning to the hearthside chair and carefully lowering the baby onto her lap. "It is a beautiful afternoon. Put on your cap and step outside. Breathe some fresh air. It will refresh you, Daughter."

"I do not feel like breathing fresh air," Susannah snapped.

I might see Edward, she thought, her heart skipping a beat at the idea.

And what would I do if I saw him again? What would I say?

She could feel her face redden in shame.

I was such a fool.

Struggling to hold back the tears, Susannah picked up another potato.

The door burst open without warning.

Susannah and her mother both cried out in surprise as two village men stepped into the room, grim expressions on their faces.

"What—?" Martha Goode started, but her voice caught in her throat.

The baby opened his eyes and gazed up at her, startled.

The two men stepped to the center of the room, revealing Benjamin Fier in the open doorway.

"My husband is not home," Martha Goode told the two officers. "I believe he is at the commons."

The two men stood stiffly, their expressions set, as Benjamin Fier strode into the room. His black boots clonked heavily on the floorboards, his face red beneath his tall black hat. "We are not here for your husband, Martha Goode," he said coldly in his booming baritone.

"I do not understand—" she replied, alarm creeping into her voice.

The baby uttered a squawk, preparing to cry. Martha Goode pulled him close to her chest. "What business have you with me, Magistrate Fier?" she asked, climbing reluctantly to her feet.

Benjamin Fier ignored her question. "Keep watch on them," he instructed the two men. "I will search for the proof."

"Proof? Proof of what?" Susannah cried, tossing down her knife and jumping to her feet. "Why are you here? Why can you not wait for my father to return?"

Benjamin ignored Susannah, too. He strode quickly to the hearth, his black cloak sweeping behind him. "Aha!" He bent down, as if picking up something from behind a kettle.

When he turned around to face them, Benjamin held a purple cloth bag in one hand. His lips spread into an unpleasant smile. "I believe we have the proof we need."

"Proof of *what?*" Susannah demanded shrilly.

Benjamin walked quickly to the table and overturned the bag, spilling its contents onto the tabletop.

To her astonishment, Susannah saw a chicken's foot, some feathers, dried roots of some kind, a small bone, and a glass vial containing a blood-colored liquid.

"What *is* that?" Susannah cried.

"That does not belong to us!" her mother cried, her

face pale, her troubled eyes darting from the items on the table to Benjamin Fier.

"We have the proof we need," Benjamin told his men, holding up the empty bag. He gestured to Susannah and her mother. "Take them to the prison. Tie them securely to await their trial."

"Trial?" Martha Goode shrieked, holding her baby tightly against her chest. "Trial for what crime?"

"For the crime of witchcraft!" Benjamin Fier declared, eyeing Susannah coldly.

The two officers moved quickly, grabbing Susannah and her mother firmly by the shoulders. Benjamin strode quickly to the door, still gripping the empty purple bag.

"Benjamin Fier—you *know* us!" Martha Goode cried desperately. "You know we are a God-fearing, humble, and pious family!"

"You cannot do this!" Susannah shrieked, fear choking her throat. "You cannot do this to us!"

The officers dragged Susannah and her mother to the door. The baby whimpered in confused fear, one tiny pink hand breaking free of his mother's grasp and thrashing the air wildly.

As Susannah and her mother were pulled out the door, Benjamin Fier stepped back to watch. His eyes gazed hard at Martha Goode, then lingered for a long while on Susannah.

He didn't smile. His face was set in rigid coldness.

But Susannah thought she caught a gleam of merriment in his dark eyes.

Just then their neighbor, Mary Halsey, attracted by the commotion, appeared at their door.

"Please take the child," Martha pleaded, and handed the baby to Mary. "Keep him safe."

The baby's whimpers turned to frightened cries.

As the two men dragged Susannah and her mother away, Benjamin Fier followed close behind, his eyes on Susannah all the while.

This is not happening, Susannah thought, her heart pounding, the blood pulsing at her temples. This cannot be happening to us.

She heard surprised murmurs as they passed through the commons. Whispered questions. Muffled cries of surprise.

The prison loomed ahead, a low clapboard building behind the meetinghouse.

"Why are you doing this to us?" Susannah cried, the words bursting from her throat. "Why are you dragging us from our home?"

Benjamin Fier stopped on the path. His voice was low and steady. His eyes locked onto Susannah's.

"You two witches will burn before the week is out," he said.

Chapter
6

———

Torches were hung on the meetinghouse walls. Their flames flickered and threatened to go out every time the door was pulled open, allowing a gust of wind into the hot room.

In the prisoners' box at the front of the court, Susannah gripped her mother's hand and stared at the flames. Her mother's hand felt so small, like that of a cold, frightened animal.

Without realizing it, Susannah had nervously started chewing her lower lip. Now she felt the bitter taste of blood in her mouth.

They burn witches, she thought, staring at the torchlight.

They've burned three already.

Her entire body convulsed in a shudder of fear. She squeezed her mother's hand tighter. Even though witches in other parts of Massachusetts Colony were hanged, Benjamin Fier believed that burning was the only way to punish a witch.

But I am not a witch!

Surely if there is justice in Wickham, I will not be found guilty.

The long, low-ceilinged room was filled with shadows. Solemn faces flickered in the orange torchlight. Eyes, dozens of eyes, peered at Susannah and her mother.

The rows of wooden benches stretched to the back of the long room. People crowded quietly into them, the frightened citizens of the town, whispering their fears, staring at Susannah and her mother with curiosity and surprise and pity.

The whispers and hushed voices grew louder, until Susannah wanted to cover her ears. "Mother, why do they stare at us like that?" she uttered in a frightened voice, leaning so close she could feel her mother's trembling. "They know us. They know who we are."

"Some believe they are staring into the faces of evil," Martha Goode replied, squeezing her daughter's hand.

"But they *know* us!" Susannah repeated shrilly, her heart thudding in her chest.

"Our innocence will soon free us," her mother replied softly. Her words were brave, but her entire body shook with fear.

Edward, where are you? Susannah wondered.

Have you spoken to your father? Have you told him about us?

"Edward will not let us burn," Susannah said out loud without realizing it.

Her mother stared at her in surprise. "What did you say?"

Susannah started to reply, but someone in a front bench cried out loudly.

Susannah heard a flapping sound and felt a cold ripple of wind close to her ear.

Startled voices called out.

Susannah heard the flapping again, like the beating of wings. A shadowy form darted overhead.

"A bat!" a man shouted from the back of the room.

The creature swooped low toward the flickering light of a torch, then flew over the prisoners' box again, its wings beating like a frightened heart.

Matthew Fier appeared at the front of the room. "Open the doors! Let it out!" he ordered.

The bat swung low over the spectators, and Susannah saw several heads duck. She felt a cool ripple of air as the bat flew past her face.

"Hold open the doors. It will fly out," Matthew Fier said in his high-pitched voice.

The doors were obediently pulled open. The torches flickered and bent in the invading breeze. A moment later the bat swooped out, disappearing into the starless sky. The doors were closed.

Matthew Fier shouted over the buzz of voices, calling for silence. He served as trial warden, keeping order during his brother's trial proceedings.

He did not have Benjamin's booming deep voice. He was not as large or imposing as his brother, but he had the same fire of ambition in his dark eyes.

The room grew silent. The shuffling of feet made the floorboards creak. Someone near the doors coughed loudly.

Matthew turned to the prisoners, adjusting the white stock he wore over his robe. "You may summon as many evil creatures as you wish," he told Susannah and her mother, his eyes glowing like dark coals. "You may summon bats or snakes—or the Evil One himself. But it will only serve to prove your guilt."

"We did not summon that bat!" Susannah cried.

"Silence!" Matthew ordered. "Silence! A dark creature like that would not enter our court unless summoned!"

Loud murmurs burst forth from the rows of benches. Accusing eyes, reflecting the torchlight, glared at Susannah and her mother.

"Silence! Silence!" Matthew shouted, gesturing with both hands.

As the room grew quiet, Susannah saw a man at the end of a row rise to his feet. "Release my wife and daughter!" he demanded.

"It is Father!" Susannah cried to her mother, leaning forward to see him better.

"Release them, Matthew Fier! You know they are not witches!" Mr. Goode cried passionately.

A tall man in dark robes strode to the front of the room and stood beside Matthew Fier. "Be seated, William Goode," Benjamin Fier ordered. "We do not place innocent women on trial here."

"But *they* are innocent!" William declared. "I swear it by all that is holy!"

"Be seated!" Benjamin commanded in his booming voice. "Be seated, William, or I will remove you from this court."

Susannah saw her father open his mouth to protest. But he uttered only a helpless groan before slumping onto his seat.

Benjamin Fier turned to face the accused. His straight black hair and dark eyes glowed almost red in the torchlight.

"Martha Goode, do you wish to confess your guilt?" he asked, leaning close to the prisoners' box.

Susannah's mother cleared her throat. Her voice came out in a choked whisper: "I have no guilt to confess."

Sneering, Benjamin turned his harsh gaze on Susannah. "Susannah Goode, do you wish to confess your guilt?"

Susannah clasped her trembling hands tightly in her lap and lowered her head, a couple of blond ringlets falling loose from her cap, over her face. "I am not a witch," she managed to mutter.

Edward, where are you?

Edward, aren't you going to save us?

Isn't anyone going to save us?

"Confess now," Benjamin demanded. "There are witnesses. Witnesses in this hall tonight. Witnesses who saw you both dancing with the Evil One in the moonlit woods."

"That is not true!" Susannah shrieked, on her feet now.

"Susannah—!" She could hear her mother's warning, feel her mother's touch on her sleeve.

"That is not true!" Susannah repeated. "We have never—"

"Be silent, witch!" Matthew Fier commanded, stepping up beside his brother, a fierce scowl on his slender face. "You have already tried to bedevil us by summoning that creature of the night into our meeting hall. Do not disrupt the trial again!"

"Confess now," Benjamin urged. "Your hollow protests only serve to demonstrate your guilt."

"But we are *innocent!*" Susannah shrieked.

"Release them! Release them now!" Susannah heard her father cry.

Low murmurs spread through the long rows of benches, growing to a roar.

"Release my innocent wife and child!" William Goode cried desperately. "My son needs his mother!"

Matthew turned to point to Susannah's father, who stood with his hat gripped tightly in one hand. "Remove him from the hall!" he shouted angrily.

Suddenly John Halsey, Mary Halsey's husband, stood in the back of the meeting house.

"Let him speak, Matthew. You've known the Goode family for years," he cried.

"Release my family!" William insisted. "This trial is a mistake! A mockery!"

"Remove him!" Matthew ordered, silencing John Halsey.

From out of the shadows two militia officers moved quickly, pushing their way into William's row, grabbing him by the shoulders.

Staring over the startled, silent faces of the onlookers, Susannah saw her father struggle. She heard angry shouts. Scuffling. A hard blow, followed by her father's cry of pain.

A few moments later she could see her father's limp body being dragged up the aisle. The doors at the back were flung open.

The sudden breeze threatened to extinguish the torches against the walls. The flames dipped low. The darkness deepened. Then the flames rose up again.

The room returned to heavy silence.

Her father had been taken out.

You cannot save us, Father, Susannah thought, cold dread tightening her throat.

You cannot save us. So who will?

Will it be you, Edward?

Are you here? Will you speak to your father? Will you rescue us from the fire?

Or will you betray me again?

"We have all witnessed their dark powers," Benjamin Fier announced to the rows of onlookers. "We have seen them try to darken this hall just now. The torches nearly went out. But our goodness prevailed over their evil power!"

He turned to Susannah and her mother. "Your evil could not douse our torches. Your evil could not put out the light of truth in this room!"

"It was the wind that nearly doused the torches!" Susannah cried.

"Silence, witch!" Benjamin screamed, his booming voice ringing off the dark wood walls.

He raised one hand high above his head. Susannah saw that his hand was gripping the purple bag, bulging with its odd assortment of items.

"I found the proof of your blasphemy!" Benjamin declared. "I myself found the tools of your witchcraft. I found this near your hearth, a hearth made cold by the presence of the Evil One!"

"It does not belong to us!" Susannah screamed, feeling her mother's restraining hand on her sleeve once again.

"Silence!" Benjamin warned, his dark eyes narrowing at Susannah.

"We have the proof of your evil practices," Benjamin continued. "We have witnesses who have seen your moonlight dance with the Evil One and his servants. And we have seen your attempts to frighten us tonight by bringing a bat into our meeting hall and trying to douse our light."

"No!" Susannah shrieked, tugging at the sides of her hair with both hands. "No! No!"

"Good shall always triumph," Benjamin continued, ignoring Susannah's shrill cries of protest. "Good shall always triumph over the Evil One. Those of us with pure hearts shall always triumph over your kind, Martha and Susannah Goode."

Susannah's mother lowered her head, but Susannah could see her shoulders trembling and knew her mother was crying.

Susannah wanted to scream out her protest, to declare her innocence until Benjamin Fier would listen to her. But she could see that her shouts were of no use.

Her heart pounding, her head spinning, Susannah slumped over and leaned her head against her mother's trembling shoulder.

"A dark evil has descended on Wickham," Benjamin Fier was saying. "As magistrate, it is my duty to battle it wherever it may appear."

He faced the onlookers and lowered his voice as he spoke to them. "It is not my desire to put on trial the wives and daughters of our village. But it is my *sacred duty* to protect all who are innocent from those possessed by the Evil One, such as these." He pointed to Susannah and her mother.

"There is nothing left but for you to confess!" he demanded, stepping up before the prisoners' box. "Do you confess, Mistress Goode? Do you confess to your evil practices?"

Susannah's mother was crying too hard to reply, her shoulders heaving, her face turned away into the shadows.

"Do you confess to practicing the dark arts, Susannah Goode?" Benjamin demanded.

"I am innocent," Susannah uttered in a choked whisper.

"Your refusal to confess," Benjamin shouted, "your unwillingness to confess to the truth *proves* your guilt!"

He stood over Susannah and her mother, leaning close, so close that Susannah could smell his sour breath. "We have found you, Martha Goode, and you, Susannah Goode, guilty of witchcraft. It is my duty as magistrate to sentence you both."

"No—please!" Susannah shrieked, reaching out to him.

He backed away, eyeing her coldly, his face half hidden in shadow. "You both shall burn tomorrow night," Benjamin announced without any emotion at all.

A pale half moon, poking through wisps of dark cloud, cast a faint rectangle of light through the tiny window of the prison cell. Susannah leaned against the cold wall and stared down at the patch of light on the dirt floor. Her hands were tied behind her, so she could do no witchery, the warden at the jail had told her.

Martha Goode lay in darkness against the opposite wall. Breathing hard, uttering low moans, calling out for her baby, she slept fitfully.

Too frightened and upset to sleep, Susannah suddenly saw a shadow making its way up the front of her skirt. A spider.

She bent toward it, struggling to free her hands. But they were fastened tightly. She could not brush the spider away. She could only stare at it helplessly as it made its way up her dress.

Outside, the white moonlight fell on two large mounds of straw, golden under the pale wash of light.

Is this the straw we will burn in? Susannah thought with a shudder.

Are these mounds of straw waiting to be our final bed?

The spider was up to her waist, its legs moving quickly over the coarse fabric of the dress.

As she stared at the mounds of straw and pictured them afire, a strangled sob burst from her throat.

She turned her eyes from the window.

I am not a witch, she thought with fierce bitterness.
My mother is not a witch.

*What of the three who have already burned? Were
they innocent, too?*

*Are the innocent burning in Wickham? Can that be
true?*

Suddenly the moonlight appeared to be snuffed out.
The tiny cell was cast in deep darkness.

Startled, Susannah turned to see a silhouette on the
other side of the window, blocking the light.

"Wh-who's there?" she stammered.

"Susannah," came a hoarse whisper.

"Edward!" she cried, feeling a burst of joy lighten
her chest. "Edward—have you come to save us?"

Chapter
7

Edward Fier stared at her, his face half hidden in darkness.

"Have you come to save us?" Susannah repeated in an eager whisper.

Edward hesitated. Susannah could see his dark eyes staring in at her, studying her coldly. "Save you? Why would I save you?" he demanded finally, his voice as cold as his eyes.

"Edward, I thought—"

"How could you betray me like this?" Edward asked, spitting the words angrily.

Susannah gasped. "Betray *you?* Edward, I did nothing to betray you. *You* betrayed *me*. You toyed with my heart. You were engaged to be married, and yet you continued to—"

"I was never engaged!" Edward insisted vehemently

in a low whisper. He pulled back from the window and glanced quickly from side to side. When he was certain there was no one around, he pressed his face close to the opening again.

"I was never engaged. I told my father that I was in love with *you!*" Edward told her bitterly.

Susannah swallowed hard. "You did?"

"But you betrayed me, Susannah."

"No. I never—" Susannah started.

"You betrayed me with the Evil One!" Edward accused, his dark eyes glowing with anger.

"No! I am innocent, Edward!" Susannah whispered fiercely. "You must believe me! You *must!*"

"You cannot be innocent," Edward whispered. "You are a witch, Susannah. You tried to lead me astray. But your evil was exposed in time."

"No! I am innocent!" Susannah declared. "Edward, you *know* me. We have been so close. We have meant so much to each other. How—" Her voice caught in her throat. She took a deep breath and tried again. "How can you be so certain of my guilt?"

He stared at her, his features set, his eyes as cold as his words. "I told you, Susannah. I revealed my feelings about you to my father. I told my father of my love for you. Do you think that knowing this, my father would put you on trial if you were innocent?"

"But, Edward—"

"Do you think my father would put me through this pain? Do you think my father would *hurt* me like this? Deliberately hurt me by trying an innocent girl?" Edward shook his head, his eyes still burning accusations into Susannah's.

"No, Susannah," he said sadly. "My father may be stern and hard, but he always does what is right. He is a good man. My father cares about me, about my feelings. He would never do this to me. He would never put you on trial unless he was certain of your guilt!"

"I swear to you, Edward—" Susannah started.

But he wouldn't let her finish. "To think that I defied my father on your behalf," Edward cried. "To think that I went against my father's wishes in order to stand up for you. To think that I risked my father's goodwill, my father, who is a good and pious man, who only wants the best for me. To think that I was ready to defy him, for *you*—a witch!"

"Edward, your father is *wrong!*" Susannah shouted desperately.

His eyes narrowed. He lowered his voice to an icy whisper. "Do not speak of my father, witch. Your spell over me is ended."

"Edward, no! Edward, please!" Susannah wailed.

The face in the window was gone. The pale moonlight returned.

Susannah sobbed quietly. Across the room her mother stirred but didn't awaken.

Susannah felt the spider inching along her neck now. Her skin tingled as it made a path up to her chin.

Go ahead, spider. Bite, she thought with a bitter sigh of defeat.

Go ahead and bite.

Across the village in the Goodes' small house, William Goode sat hunched in a tall-backed chair.

The fire had burned low, purple embers sizzling quietly. The room grew cold. William, staring blankly at the darkening hearth, didn't notice.

Deep in despair, he had been sitting motionless for more than an hour. Unable to focus his eyes, unable to focus his mind. The sounds of the trial, the shadowy faces, and the accusing eyes all washed across his distressed mind.

All is lost, he thought, picturing his wife and daughter, picturing them at home by the fire, picturing them in the peace and tranquillity that would never return. Even his baby was lost to him—a neighbor had George for the time being.

All is lost.

When a knock came at the door, William didn't move.

Sinking deeper and deeper into his despair, he didn't hear it.

The knock repeated. And then again even more loudly, a third time.

William stirred, raised his head, listened.

Yes. A knock on the door.

Who could it be at this hour? Who would have the nerve to come to his door, knowing how he must be suffering at this moment?

Knowing how he would suffer the rest of his life. How this night would be played out again and again in his mind until the day he died.

The loud knocking was repeated.

Someone was being very insistent.

With a groan William pulled himself unsteadily to his feet.

The purple embers came into focus.

The fire is dying, he thought.

Everything in my life is dying.

More loud knocking.

"Go away," William muttered.

But he made his way to the door and pulled it open.

The bright light of a torch caused William to shield his eyes. Slowly the face of the torch bearer came into view.

"Matthew Fier! What do you want of me?" William demanded weakly. "Have you come to take me away too?"

Chapter
8

The torchlight fell over Matthew Fier's face, casting it into deep shadow. His dark eyes stared out at William, black circles ringed by black as black as the grave.

"I have come to help you, not accuse you, William," Matthew said softly. He raised the torch high, and once again his face disappeared under the shadow of his hat.

"Help me?" William asked weakly, his body sagging in the narrow doorway.

"May I come in?"

William nodded and took a step back. Matthew Fier set the torch down in the dirt and edged into the house, pulling his cloak around him. He removed his hat, revealing tousled brown hair. He hung the hat on a hook on the wall.

The two men stood awkwardly in front of the door, staring at each other.

William was the first to break the silence. "My wife and daughter have been unjustly accused. Your brother has made a dreadful mistake. Martha and Susannah know nothing of the dark arts."

Matthew started to move past William, his eyes on the dying fire. But William grabbed the front of his cloak. "Your brother is wrong!" he cried. "He is wrong! Wrong!"

"My brother is human," Matthew said softly. He pulled away from William's grasp and, straightening the front of his cloak, stepped to the fire.

William stared after him, bewildered by his remark.

Matthew picked up a log from beside the fireplace and dropped it onto the dying embers. "You let your fire die, William," he said, staring into the hearth.

"I do not care about fires now," William replied, his trembling voice revealing his emotion. "I care only about my wife and daughter. I implore you, Matthew—"

Matthew turned to face William, clasping his hands in front of his gray doublet. He had rough hands, William saw. Farmer's hands.

"I believe I can help you, William," Matthew said slowly, softly.

"You mean—?"

"I believe I can save your wife and daughter."

William uttered a loud sigh. He gestured to the straight-backed chair near the fire.

Matthew shook his head. He began to pace back and forth in front of the hearth, his boots clicking against the floorboards. "My brother is human, as I said."

William scratched his white hair. "I do not understand. Do you mean to say . . ." His voice trailed off.

"I have influence with Benjamin," Matthew said, raising his dark eyes to William's.

"You can talk to him?" William asked eagerly. "You can reason with him? You can explain to him that he has made a tragic error?"

A strange smile formed on Matthew's face. He stopped pacing and nodded. "I believe I can persuade my brother to change the verdict. Your wife and daughter need not burn tomorrow evening."

"Oh, thank you! Thank you, Matthew!" William cried joyfully. He dropped to his knees and bowed his head in a silent prayer.

When he raised his eyes, he saw that Matthew still had a strange smile on his lips. A wave of doubt swept over William as he climbed heavily to his feet. "You really can sway your brother?" he asked hopefully. "Your brother will listen to you?"

Matthew nodded. Sweeping his cloak around him, he lowered himself into the tall-backed wooden chair. "I can persuade Benjamin," he repeated. He narrowed his dark eyes. "But it will be costly."

"What?" William wasn't certain he had heard correctly. Was Matthew Fier asking for payment? For a bribe?

"It will be costly, William," Matthew repeated, his smile fading. "My services in this matter must be well rewarded."

William Goode swallowed hard. "I have little money," he choked out. "But I will spend every shilling I have to save Martha and Susannah."

"The price is one hundred pounds," Matthew announced flatly, staring hard at William.

"One hundred pounds?" William cried, unable to conceal his surprise. "But, Matthew, I beg you!"

"One hundred pounds is a small price to pay," Matthew said, rising and walking over to the hearth. The fresh log had just caught flame. Matthew held out his hands to warm them.

William gaped at him in disbelief.

He is willing to spare Martha and Susannah in exchange for a bribe, William thought. I knew the Fier brothers were ambitious. I knew their characters were weakened by the sin of greed. But I never dreamed they were *so* corrupt. I never dreamed they would try to increase their wealth by threatening the lives of an innocent woman and girl.

"Matthew, I have only eighty pounds," William protested. "Eighty pounds is all that I brought from England, all that I possess in the world. If you take it, I will have nothing."

Matthew's dark eyes lit up, reflecting the leaping flames in the hearth. "You will have your wife and daughter," he said flatly.

William lowered his head, knowing he would pay the huge sum to Matthew Fier. Knowing he would pay *anything* to rescue Martha and Susannah from the flames.

When he looked up, Matthew was examining a long-handled pan hanging on the wall beside the hearth. "Very nice warming pan," he said, taking it down and turning it over in his hands, admiring it. "Is it brass?"

"It is of the finest brass," William replied. "It was crafted by my father."

"I will take it as part of the payment," Matthew announced, still examining it. "Since you do not have the full one hundred pounds to pay me."

"Take it," William replied with a wave of his hand. "Take everything I own, Matthew. Just return my family to me safely."

Matthew lowered the warming pan and gazed around the small room. "Speaking of your family, where is little George?" he asked.

"Mary Halsey next door has taken the baby," William replied unhappily. "He needed a nurse. And I could not bear to look upon him, to see his innocent face and know that he would grow up without ever knowing his mother or sister."

A loud sob escaped William's throat. He wiped tears from his eyes. "I will get you your payment, Matthew," he said in a voice trembling with emotion. "Then will you speak to Benjamin tonight?"

Matthew nodded solemnly. "Your family will be released tomorrow at sunset. Your troubled heart may rest easy, William."

His head still spinning, William eagerly made his way to the back of the house, where his life savings were hidden. As he pulled the heavy cloth bag up from under a loose floorboard, he felt as if his heart were about to burst.

Martha will be home tomorrow night!

Susannah will be home too!

We will all be so happy again. What rejoicing we will do!

He hoisted the bag to the front room and sat down at the table to count it out. William Fier, carrying the brass warming pan in one hand, made his way to the table and peered over William's shoulder at the large coins.

"Eighty pounds," William said finally, shoving the pile of coins toward Matthew. "I am left with two copper shillings. But I am a rich man!"

"Yes, you are," Matthew agreed, his face completely expressionless. As he leaned forward to collect the coins, the pendant he wore around his neck fell in front of William's eyes.

It was so unusual that William couldn't help but comment on it. "What an interesting amulet you wear, Matthew," he remarked.

Matthew stood up and fingered the amulet, as if seeing it for the first time.

The silver disk sparkled with blue jewels. The jewels were grasped by a silver three-toed claw. Matthew twirled the disk in his fingers. On the back three Latin words were inscribed.

William struggled to read the words: *"Dominatio per malum.*

"Quite unusual," William said. "What do the words mean?"

Matthew tucked the amulet back inside his doublet. "Just an old saying," he replied with a shrug. "The amulet was given to me by my grandmother before I left our village. I wear it only as a reminder of that wonderful old woman and of my previous life, a life of poverty and struggle."

William raised his eyes to Matthew's, studying his face in the dim firelight. "I have heard such a claw referred to as a demon's claw," he told his visitor. "It is said to have powers."

For a brief moment Matthew's mouth remained open in surprise. When he regained his composure, he said, "I know nothing about powers or demon's claws. Nor should you, William Goode."

"No, of course not," William said quickly, lowering his eyes.

Matthew Fier collected the remaining coins. Then, carrying the brass warming pan, he made his way to the door, his cloak sweeping behind him. He lowered his hat onto his head and turned to gaze back at William.

William hadn't risen from the table. His entire body was trembling. Trembling with joy. With eagerness. With relief. "My family—" he managed to say.

"I will make sure of everything," Matthew Fier promised. Then, pulling his heavy cloak closer about him, he opened the door and disappeared into the night.

Chapter
9

The next evening William Goode hurried across the commons toward the prison. A small flock of sheep interrupted their grazing to raise their heads and mutter their surprise in his direction.

The sun spread rose-colored waves across the evening sky as it lowered itself behind the trees. A pale half moon was already visible, just poking over the shingled roof of Benjamin Fier's two-story house.

The day had gone by in a haze for William. Mary Halsey had brought him his midday meal, but it had gone untouched. He had intended to mend the fence around his wife's small kitchen garden but hadn't the strength.

Time had stood still, and William Goode frozen with it.

Only when the sun had begun to sink and evening

63

approached had William sprung to life. Now he moved quickly past squawking chickens and a lowing herd of scrawny cows, eager to be reunited with his beloved family.

Eager to hug them, to touch them. Eager to share the warm tears that would flow, the happy tears that would wash away the terror, erase all of the nightmares. Eager to bring Martha and Susannah home.

As the low, gray prison building came into view, William's heart began to pound. So much joy! So much relief! Panting loudly with excitement, he slowed his pace. Then he stopped to catch his breath.

A yapping hound ran across his path. William looked up to see a crowd in front of the prison entrance.

They've come to share my joy, he realized.

Their faces were hidden from him, hidden by dark hats and hoods. But he knew they were his neighbors, his friends, grateful for the reversal of the unjust verdict, grateful for the Goodes' change of fortune.

As he approached them his knees felt weak, his legs trembly. He forced himself to take a deep breath and hold it. He could hear their murmuring voices as they huddled near the prison doorway.

This is the happiest day of my life, he thought.

And then the door swung open. An officer appeared.

Another officer stepped out in front of the murmuring crowd.

Susannah came next, her head lowered as she walked through the doorway. Martha Goode followed close behind, her shadow blue against the hard gray ground.

"Susannah! Martha!" William called, pushing eagerly through the crowd of well-wishers.

They both raised their eyes and searched for him.

"Here I am! Martha! Over here! Susannah!" William called happily. He stepped to the front of the group of onlookers, breathing hard, his face red, his vision already blurred by happy tears.

"Martha! Susannah!"

He watched for them to be released.

But to his surprise, their hands were tied behind their backs.

William gasped as one of the officers turned and shoved Martha from behind, pushing her hard, causing her to stumble forward.

"Martha!" William cried.

She saw him finally and called out to him, a mournful expression on her face.

"Do not worry!" he called. "They are releasing you now!"

"Father!" Susannah cried shrilly, her face also twisted in anguish. "Help us, Father!"

"Do not worry—" William started. But his voice caught in his throat as he saw the officers force his wife and daughter toward the low mounds of straw.

"Father—!" Susannah pleaded.

"William! William! Help us!" Martha cried.

"Wait!" William shouted.

Someone tried to restrain him. "It is all in the hands of the Maker," he heard someone mutter. "Let us pray for their souls."

"No!" William screamed. He pulled away, jerked

himself free, and began running toward them. "Stop! Stop!"

To William's horror, Susannah and Martha had already been marched to the straw piles and were being tied to tall wooden stakes.

"Nooooo!" William's scream of protest raged in the evening air like the howl of a desperate animal.

His vision blurred by angry tears, he burst forward, howling his rage, a frantic wail of protest. He stopped short when he saw Benjamin Fier at the edge of the crowd, overseeing the proceedings, hands on the sides of his long black cloak, his face hidden in the shadow of his wide-brimmed hat.

"Benjamin—!" William screamed, grabbing the magistrate from behind by the shoulders. "Benjamin —you must stop this now! Free them! Your brother promised me—!"

With a desperate sigh William spun him around by the shoulders . . . and gazed into an unexpected face.

"Giles!" William croaked, his voice a shocked whisper. "Giles Roberts!"

"William, please let go of me," the deputy magistrate said softly.

"Giles? But . . . but . . ." William stammered breathlessly, too astonished to think clearly.

Susannah and Martha were now tightly secured to the stakes. The two officers were moving forward with lighted torches.

"Stop them, Giles!" William demanded. "Stop them at once. Where is Benjamin? Where is Benjamin Fier? I must speak to him before . . . before . . ."

Giles Roberts took a step back, freeing himself from William's grip.

"William, have you not heard?" he asked, staring into William's tear-filled eyes. "Benjamin and his brother, Matthew, fled the village before dawn this morning."

Chapter
10

════════

"Fled the village?" William cried frantically, staring over Giles Roberts's shoulder to the straw piles where his wife and daughter were twisting in terror against the wooden stakes that held them.

"Before dawn," Giles repeated solemnly.

"But I paid Matthew—!" William cried. "I paid him to—"

"The Fiers robbed us," Giles told him. "They emptied the storehouse. They left us no food for winter. They took everything. Everything."

"I—I don't understand!" William cried, feeling the ground tilt and whirl beneath him. He shut his eyes, tried to steady himself.

"They loaded all their belongings onto wagons," Giles told him. "And they disappeared with all of our supplies."

"But didn't they speak to you before they left?" William demanded, desperately clutching at Giles. "Didn't Benjamin tell you? Didn't Matthew tell you?"

"They didn't speak to me, William," Giles replied softly. And then he added firmly, "Please let go of me."

"But the sentence against my wife and daughter was to be reversed! They are to be freed, Giles! Benjamin should have told you. He should have—"

"He told me nothing," Giles said. The deputy magistrate's features grew hard. "The sentence must be carried out."

There was no use struggling, Susannah realized.

Her hands were tightly bound. She could not free herself from the stake. It poked uncomfortably into her back. Her wrists throbbed against the tight cords. Her shoulders ached.

She raised her eyes to the sky. The sun had lowered itself behind the trees, the trees she had loved to walk among. The piney sweet-smelling trees that had brought her so much joy. The trees where she and Edward had hidden during their brief secret meetings, during her brief happiness.

Lowering her eyes, she thought she saw Edward.

He stood at the edge of the crowd, staring back at her.

At first Susannah saw hurt in his eyes. Pain.

But as she gazed at him, his face appeared to harden before her eyes, until it became a mask of cold hatred.

She cried out—and realized it wasn't him.

It wasn't Edward.

The boy didn't look at all like Edward.

Two circles of yellow light approached from out of the grayness.

Two torches.

"Mother—" Susannah cried. "Mother, will it hurt?"

Tears streamed down Martha Goode's swollen cheeks. She turned her face from her daughter, struggling to stifle her sobs.

"Will it hurt, Mother? Tell me, Mother—will it hurt?"

Chapter
11

William Goode pressed his hands against the sides of his face. But the anguished screams of his wife and daughter invaded his ears.

I'll hear their screams forever.

Eyes closed, he could still picture their bodies twisting on the flaming stakes, still see their melting faces, their fiery hair.

He had tried to run to them.

But the two officers had held him back, pushing him to the ground, holding him on his knees as the choking black smoke fogged the sky and the howls of agony rose higher than the flames.

Martha. Susannah.

My family . . .

William was still on his knees when the fire had

been doused and the silent crowd had departed. He hadn't noticed that he was alone now.

Alone with his grief.

Alone with the stench of the smoke in his nostrils.

Alone with the screams of his wife and daughter ringing in his ears.

They burned so brightly, he thought, sobbing.

They burned as bright as stars.

The ground beneath him was puddled with his tears.

He raised his eyes to the night sky, the color of coal, pierced with pale white stars.

I know you're both up there, William thought, climbing unsteadily to his feet.

I know you are both up there, bright as stars.

He uttered one last, wrenching sob. Then his grief quickly gave way to his fury.

He strode home through the silent, deserted commons, his eyes held straight ahead. The fire faded in his mind, faded to dark, shifting images, pictures of Benjamin and Matthew Fier.

His fury grew with every step.

Betrayed.

They betrayed me and stole my life.

"William?" A voice startled him at his front door. It took him a while to erase the hated images of the Fier brothers and focus on the dark figure in his doorway.

"Mary Halsey!" he whispered.

She held the baby up to him, wrapped tightly in a wool blanket. "Take the baby, William. Take George."

"No." William raised his hands as if to fend the baby off.

"He is your only family now," Mary Halsey insisted, thrusting the baby forward. "Take him. Hold him, William. He will help you get over your grief."

"No," William repeated. "Not now, Mary Halsey. There is something I must do first."

He startled her by pushing past her and entering his house, closing the door hard behind him.

The house was dark, nearly as dark as William's thoughts. The fire had long since burned out.

William moved quickly through the darkness to the back of the house. He pulled open the door that led to his special room, the tiny, secret room behind the wall, where even Susannah and Martha had never gone.

The room where the black candles were always lighted.

He stepped into the flickering orange light and pulled the door closed behind him.

Whispering the ancient words of the purification ritual, William removed the scarlet hooded robe from its hiding place beneath a stack of wooden boxes and pulled it around him.

William could feel the power of the robe even before he lowered the hood over his head.

Bowing his head three times, William gazed around the circle of candlelight. Then he dropped to his knees on the dirt floor and began to chant the ancient words he knew so well.

My wife and daughter were innocent, William thought bitterly as he chanted.

They were innocent.

But I am not.

They had no knowledge of these dark arts.

But I have practiced them well.

Whispering the ancient dark curses, he began to scratch signs of evil in the dirt floor. He was breathing hard now, his heart pounding in his chest.

Under the satiny scarlet hood he glared, unblinking, at the ancient symbols he was scratching in the dirt. A grim smile formed on his trembling lips.

Innocence died today, William Goode thought as he summoned the spirits of evil he had summoned so many times before.

Innocence died today. But my hatred will live for generations.

The Fiers shall not escape me.

Wherever they flee, I will be there.

My family's screams shall become the Fiers' tortured screams.

The fire that burned today will not be quenched— until revenge is mine, and the Fiers burn forever in the fire of my curse!

Village of Shadyside
1900

"That's how it began. That's how it all began more than two hundred years ago," Nora Goode said.

Staring into the yellow candle glow, she set down her pen. Her slender hand ached from writing.

How long have I been here? she wondered, allowing her eyes to trail down the melting wax on the side of the candle.

How long have I been seated at this narrow table, writing the story of my ancestors?

The candle flickered, reminding her of the fire. Once again she saw the burning mansion. Once again she heard the anguished screams of her loved ones trapped inside the blaze.

How did I escape? Nora wondered, staring intently into the flame.

I don't remember.

How did I get here?

Someone brought me here. Someone found me. Someone found me on the lawn, staring into the fire, watching the mansion burn.

Someone helped me away from there and brought me to this room.

And now I must write it all down. I must tell the whole story. I must explain about the two families and the curse that has followed us through the decades.

Nora picked up the pen. With a trembling hand she straightened up the stack of papers on the small table.

She leaned toward the smooth yellow candle flame.

I must finish the story before the night is ended, she thought.

So little time.

Susannah and Martha Goode burned in 1692. Now my story picks up eighteen years later.

Benjamin and Matthew Fier are once again successful farmers. Matthew's wife, Constance, has given him a daughter, Mary.

Benjamin's son, Edward, is a grown man. He never married Anne Ward, but he has married Rebecca, a woman from a nearby village. They have a son named Ezra.

So much to tell. So much to tell . . .

Taking a deep breath, Nora bent over the table. A few seconds later her pen scratched against the paper as she resumed her dark tale.

PART TWO

Western Pennsylvania Frontier
1710

Chapter
12

"Sometimes I think this family is cursed," Benjamin Fier muttered, pulling his chair closer to the long dining table. He shook his head unhappily, his disheveled white hair glowing in the fading evening light that filtered through the window.

"You are starting to sound like a crotchety old man, Father," Edward said, laughing.

"I *am* a crotchety old man!" Benjamin declared with pride.

"How can you say we are cursed?" Benjamin's brother, Matthew, demanded, sniffing the aroma of roast chicken as he entered the room. "Look how our farm has prospered, Benjamin. Look how our family has grown."

"I can see that *you* have certainly grown," Benjamin teased.

Matthew had become quite stout. As he took his place at the table, everyone could see that his linen shirt was stretched tight around his bulging middle.

"Uncle Benjamin, are you teasing my father again?" Mary Fier scolded. Matthew's daughter Mary set a serving platter of potatoes and string beans in front of Matthew.

"Well, don't you look like Queen Anne herself!" Benjamin roared at Mary.

Mary blushed. "I put my hair up. That is all."

Mary was seventeen. She had long copper-colored hair, as did her mother, Constance Fier. She also had her mother's creamy, pale complexion and shy smile. She had her father Matthew's dark, penetrating eyes.

"Why do you scold Mary?" Constance demanded of Benjamin, sweeping into the room, holding the platter of roast chicken in front of her long white apron. "Mary worked all afternoon, peeling potatoes and snapping the beans for your dinner."

"I also picked the beans," Mary added grumpily.

"He was only teasing, Cousin Mary," Edward said. "Weren't you, Father?"

Benjamin didn't reply. He had a faraway look clouding his dark eyes. He stared at the narrow window.

"Father?" Edward repeated.

Benjamin lowered his eyes to his son with a frown. "Were you addressing me?" he barked. "Speak up! I am an old man, Edward. I cannot abide mutterers."

"Where is Rebecca?" Matthew demanded, his eyes searching the long, narrow dining room.

Rebecca, Edward's beautiful young wife, always seemed to be the last to the table.

"I believe she is tending Ezra," Edward told his uncle.

"Your son has been trouble since the day he was born," Benjamin grumbled. His booming voice had become raspy and harsh.

"Ezra is a difficult child," Edward admitted to his father, accepting the platter of chicken. "But I believe you go too far."

"I'm his grandfather. I can go as far as I please," Benjamin bellowed unpleasantly. "If you don't like my remarks, Edward, go eat your dinner at your own house." He pointed out the window toward Edward's house across the pasture.

"Hush, Brother," Matthew instructed, raising a hand for peace. "Let us enjoy our dinner without your usual sour complaints."

Rebecca entered, pulling Ezra behind her. It was evident from Ezra's wet eyes that he'd been crying. Ezra was six but acted as if he were much younger. Rebecca, sighing wearily, lifted him into a chair and told him not to squirm.

Rebecca had straight black hair pulled back from a high forehead, olive-green eyes, and dramatic dark lips. She had been a high-spirited, giggly girl when she married Edward, but six years of mothering Ezra and helping out on the farm had brought lines to her forehead and a weariness to her voice.

"Will you eat some chicken now, Ezra?" she asked.

"No!" the boy shouted, crossing his arms defiantly in front of his chest.

"He has a strong will. He is a true Fier," Benjamin growled approvingly.

"I am not!" Ezra cried peevishly. "I am Ezra. That is all."

Everyone laughed.

Rebecca dropped a chicken leg onto the boy's plate. "Eat your dinner," she instructed softly.

"What a fine family we are," Matthew said happily, patting his large belly. "Look around this table, Benjamin. Look at our children and grandchildren. And think of our prosperous farm and trading store. How can you say this family is cursed?"

Benjamin chewed his food slowly before replying. "Cursed," he muttered after swallowing. "The new roof shingles. Edward finished putting them up just last week. And last night that thunderstorm washed away half of them. Is that not a curse?"

Edward chuckled. "Only a few shingles were blown off, Father," he said, reaching for his pewter water cup. "There will still be light after dinner. I will go up on the roof and examine it closely. I am certain it is but a minor repair."

"Cousin Edward, it will be too dark," Mary warned. "Can it not wait until tomorrow?"

Mary and Edward were more like brother and sister than cousins. Mary was also close to Edward's wife Rebecca. There were few young people in the village for Mary to befriend. She had only her family to turn to for companionship.

"There will be enough light to examine the shingles," Edward assured her, helping himself to more string beans. He smiled at Mary. "Do not fret. Wipe your uncle's words from your mind. There is no curse on the Fier family. The only curse around here is my crotchety old father!"

The family's laughter rose up from the long dining table. It floated out the window, out of the two-story stone house to reach the ears of a white-bearded man in ragged clothes who was hidden behind the fat trunk of an old oak tree just beyond Mary's small flower garden.

Careful to keep out of view, the man leaned toward the sound of laughter, the sleeve of his worn coat pressed against the rough bark. His tired eyes explored the steep shingled roof of the sturdy farmhouse. Then he lowered his gaze to the window where the tangy aroma of roast chicken floated out.

The man's stomach growled. It had been a while since he had eaten.

But he was too excited to think about food now.

Too excited to think about his long journey. A journey of years.

He could feel his heart pound beneath his thin shirt. His breath escaped in noisy wheezes—such rapid breathing his sides began to ache. He gripped the tree trunk so tightly his hands hurt.

"At last!" he whispered to the tree. "At last!" A whispered cry of joy, of triumph.

The white-haired man was William Goode.

For almost twenty years I have sought this moment, he thought, staring intently at the flickering light through the window, listening to the chime of voices inside.

For twenty years I have searched the colonies for the Fiers, my enemies.

At last I have found them.

At last I can carry out my curse. At last I can avenge my wife and daughter.

I have found the Fiers. And now they will suffer as I have suffered. All of them. One by one.

He heard the clatter of dishes, the scrape of chairs.

Then, to his surprise, the door opened and a young man came out of the house, followed by several others.

With a gasp William pulled his head back out of view and pressed himself even tighter against the tree's ragged bark. The sun was low behind the trees. The sky was a wash of pink and purple, quickly darkening.

From his hiding place, William Goode squinted hard, struggling to recognize the faces of those he had hunted for so many years.

He had somehow expected them to look the same. Now he stared in surprise to see the changed faces and bodies.

Can that be Edward Fier? he asked himself, watching the young man prop a wooden ladder against the side of the house. Edward was but a boy when last I saw him. Now he has become a sturdy young man.

And that white-haired man, stooped over his walking stick? William squinted hard. Can *that* be Benjamin Fier?

He has aged badly, William decided. Back in Wickham he was tall and broad-shouldered, a man as powerful as his booming voice. And now his shoulders are hunched, and he leans heavily on his stick with a trembling grip.

All the better to help you topple into your grave, Benjamin Fier, William Goode thought with a grim smile.

I still have my powers, William thought with satisfaction. And I plan to use them now.

Recognizing Benjamin's brother, Matthew, William nearly laughed out loud. Why, he has become as fat as one of his cows! William declared to himself. Look how he struts with his belly hanging out.

You will strut to your grave, Matthew, William decided, feeling a wave of bitterness sweep over him. It will be a painful journey for you, Matthew. You will beg for death. But I will make your death agonizing and slow. For you are my betrayer. You are the one who robbed me of my money—and my family!

William couldn't have known the little boy who was scampering through the flower garden, unheedful of the blossoming flowers. Nor did he recognize the copper-haired young woman who held the side of the ladder.

What fine linen shirts the men all wear, thought William bitterly. And the girl's dress is of the most expensive fabric.

What are the young people's names? Are they the children or the grandchildren of the Fier brothers?

It doesn't matter, he thought, closing his eyes, a broad smile hidden behind his scraggly mustache and beard. It doesn't matter what your names are. You are Fiers.

And all Fiers shall start to suffer now.

All.

Chapter
13

"The sun is nearly down," Mary told her cousin, gripping the sides of the ladder.

"There is enough light," Edward insisted. "Move away. I am only going up for a moment."

"But the shingles are still wet from the rain," Mary insisted. "Wait until morning, Edward."

"Please. I shall be down in a moment," Edward said stubbornly. "Why do you always treat me as if I'm Ezra's age, Mary?"

"Why do you always insist on being so reckless?" Mary replied. "It's as if you have to show off to Uncle Benjamin and my father. You have nothing to prove to them, Edward."

"Maybe I have things to prove to myself," Edward muttered. "Now, please, Cousin—allow me to make my inspection of the shingles before the moon is up."

Mary obediently took a step back. "May I hold the ladder in place for you?" she asked as Edward began to climb.

"You know you should be in the kitchen helping Rebecca and your mother clean the dinner dishes."

Mary groaned and rolled her eyes. "I am seventeen, Cousin Edward," she said sharply. "I am not a girl. I am a woman."

"Your place is still in the kitchen," Edward called down. He had reached the roof and was edging his way off the ladder. "It appears much steeper up here than it did down on the ground," he said.

Mary backed up a few paces to see him better. The sun had disappeared. Edward was a dark figure against an even darker sky.

"Please be careful!" Mary called. "You're up so high, and it's so dark, and—"

Her voice caught in her throat as Edward's arms shot up. She saw his legs buckle and his body tilt.

And then she opened her mouth wide and began to scream as she realized Edward was falling, falling headfirst to the ground.

Chapter
14

Edward hit the ground with a sickening crack.

The horrifying sound split the air, louder than Mary's screams.

A second later another scream burst from the house.

Matthew came hurrying from the toolhouse at the end of the garden, followed by Benjamin, hobbling as fast as he could with his walking stick.

Rebecca was the first from the house, with Constance right behind her.

Mary, her hands pressed against her face, hurried to Edward, diving beside him on the dark ground. "Edward—?"

He gazed up at her lifelessly, a startled expression frozen on his face.

"Edward—?"

He blinked. Swallowed hard. Took a noisy, deep breath.

"My arm—" he whispered.

Mary lowered her gaze to his left arm buried beneath his body at an unnatural angle. She gasped.

"I—I can't move it," Edward whispered.

"You broke it," Mary told him, gently placing a hand on his chest.

"What happened?" Benjamin cried breathlessly, still struggling to get to the house.

"Is Edward injured?" Matthew demanded.

"Edward, can you get up?" Constance asked softly.

Mary turned and raised her eyes to her mother and Rebecca. "Oh, Mother!" she cried in horror, her mouth dropping open in disbelief.

The front of Constance's dress was splattered with blood.

"I—I—" Constance lowered her gaze. She held up her hand. Blood poured down her arm.

"I was cleaning the carving knife when I heard you scream, Mary," she explained. "The sound startled me. The knife slipped, and—" She hesitated. "I shall be fine. I just—"

"Let us get you into the house!" Mary cried, jumping to her feet. "We have to stop the bleeding."

As Mary led her mother back to the kitchen, Matthew and Rebecca lifted Edward to his feet. With his good arm around Rebecca's shoulders, Edward took a few unsteady steps.

"I think I can walk," Edward said, his jaw clenched against the pain. "But my arm . . . it is badly broken, I fear."

Leaning heavily on his walking stick, Benjamin Fier watched them walk off, shaking his head. "Cursed," he growled to himself. "The whole family is cursed."

The harsh crowing of roosters woke Mary at dawn. Gray light filtered through her tiny bedroom window. The air in the room felt hot and heavy.

She pulled herself up slowly, not at all rested. The back of her shift stuck to her skin.

What a horrid night, she thought, stretching, her shoulders aching. I don't think I slept an entire hour. I just kept picturing Edward lying on the ground in a heap. I kept hearing the crack as his arm broke. And I kept seeing the blood pouring down Mother's arm.

I tied Mother's wrist as tightly as I could. But it seemed to take forever to stop the flow of blood.

Meanwhile, Edward howled in pain as Matthew struggled to set the broken arm. Ezra was screaming and crying in the corner. Poor Rebecca didn't know which of her family to comfort—Edward or Ezra?

Finally a sling was fashioned for Edward from a bolt of heavy linen. Rebecca led her family back to their house, Ezra's frightened wails ringing through the air.

What an unfortunate night.

Mary lowered her feet to the floor, then made her way to the dresser, squinting against the gray light.

Why do I have this feeling? she wondered. Why do I have this dark feeling that our bad luck isn't over?

* * *

Mary returned from the henhouse after breakfast, a large basket of white and brown eggs pressed against the front of her long white apron.

The sun was just climbing above the trees, but the air was already hot and sticky. Puffy clouds hovered overhead. A rooster crowed. Somewhere in the direction of the barn a dog barked in reply.

Mary walked with her head lowered, her copper hair flowing down her back nearly to the waist of her linen dress.

She nearly dropped the egg basket when a strange voice behind her called out, "Good morning, miss!"

Uttering a short cry of surprise, Mary spun around and stared into the sky blue eyes of a smiling young man. He grinned at her, his eyes lighting up as if enjoying her surprise.

"Oh. H-hello," Mary stammered. "I didn't see you."

She realized she was staring at him. He was a good-looking boy, about her age, maybe a year or two older. Above his sparkling blue eyes he had heavy blond eyebrows on a broad, tanned forehead. The skin beside his eyes crinkled when he smiled. He had wavy blond hair the color of butter, which fell heavily down to his collar.

He wore a loose-fitting white shirt, the front open nearly to his waist, over Indian-style deerskin breeches. His boots were worn and covered with dust.

"I am sorry to trouble you," he said, still grinning, his eyes locked on hers. "I am looking for the owner of this farm."

"That would be my father," Mary replied, turning her gaze to the house. "Matthew Fier."

"Is your father around?" the young man asked, the morning sunlight making his blond hair glow golden.

"I believe so. Follow me," Mary replied shyly.

He reached out and took the egg basket from her. "I'll carry it for you," he said, smiling pleasantly at her. "It looks heavy."

"I carry it every morning," Mary protested, but she allowed him to take the basket. "We have a lot of chickens."

"It's a very big farm," the boy said, gesturing to the far pasture with his free hand. His boots crunched loudly over the hard ground. "My father and I settled here recently. We live in a small cabin outside the village. I don't think I've ever seen a farm this big."

Mary smiled awkwardly. "My father and uncle came here before I was born. The farm has been growing ever since."

"What is your name, miss?" the boy asked boldly, his blue eyes flashing.

Before Mary could answer, Matthew appeared, lumbering out the back door. His flannel shirt hung loose over his big belly. His knee breeches had a stain on one knee.

Matthew yawned loudly and stretched his hands over his head. Then he noticed the young man holding the egg basket beside Mary.

"Oh," Matthew said, furrowing his brow and clearing his throat. "And who might you be?"

Matthew's brusqueness didn't seem to bother the

young man. "Good morning," he said with a confident smile. "My name is Jeremy Thorne, sir."

"And what might your business be, Jeremy Thorne?" Matthew asked. "Has Mary hired you to be her egg carrier?"

Jeremy laughed even though Matthew's remark wasn't terribly funny. "No, sir," he replied cheerfully. "But I have come to your farm in search of work."

Matthew Fier stared rather unpleasantly at Jeremy. "I regret to say I'm not looking for farm help right now," he told Jeremy. "If you would kindly—"

Matthew was interrupted by Edward, perspiring from his walk across the pasture from his house. "Wait a moment, Uncle Matthew!" Edward cried. He raised his free hand to halt the conversation.

Startled, Matthew turned to his nephew. "Good morning, Nephew. Does the arm give much pain this morning?"

"Enough," Edward replied dryly, glancing at his arm, suspended in the sling. "I overheard your conversation with this young man, Uncle Matthew. I believe we do need an extra hand."

He gestured to his heavy sling. "You have lost my services for a while," Edward continued. "I believe this boy's timing is perfect. He can take some of my tasks—until my arm is healed."

Matthew rubbed his chins thoughtfully, his eyes trained on Jeremy. "Maybe . . ." he muttered reluctantly. "Where do you come from, boy?"

"From the village," Jeremy replied, eyeing Edward's sling. "My father and I settled here recently. My father is ill, sir. I am our sole support."

"No sad stories, please," Matthew cut him off, still rubbing his many chins. Matthew studied him. "You look strong enough."

Jeremy raised himself to his full height, throwing back his broad, muscular shoulders. "Yes, sir," he said quietly.

Mary stood stiffly, watching them all. She wanted to urge her father to hire Jeremy, but she knew better than to utter a word. It was not her place.

Matthew nodded. "All right, Jeremy Thorne. You may begin by cleaning out that toolhouse." He pointed to the low wooden structure behind the garden. "Pull all of the equipment out. We plan to build a bigger one."

"Thank you, sir!" Jeremy exclaimed happily. "I am very grateful. And my pay?"

"Ten shillings a week," Matthew replied quickly. "But let us see what kind of worker you are before we begin to think of you as more than temporary help."

"Very good, sir," Jeremy said. He glanced quickly at Mary.

She felt a shiver at the back of her neck.

He's so good-looking, she thought, lowering her eyes to the ground.

All kinds of thoughts raced through her mind, surprising thoughts, exciting thoughts.

But of course Father would never approve of anything between a mere farmhand and me, she realized, stopping the flow of wild thoughts in midstream.

Jeremy Thorne.

Jeremy. Jeremy. Jeremy.

She couldn't stop his name from repeating in her mind.

Her heart pounding, Mary took the egg basket from Jeremy and hurried to the house.

The talk at lunch was of the dreadful mishaps of the night before. Poor Edward. Poor Constance.

They all lowered their heads in prayer before starting their soup.

Mary couldn't stop thinking about Jeremy.

All morning long as she'd done her many kitchen chores, she had sneaked peeks at him from the door. She saw that he was proving to be as hard a worker as he had claimed.

At the back of the garden she could see the pile of tools and heavy equipment he had dragged out of the toolhouse. She watched him working alone back there, lowering his head to enter the structure, then appearing again with another handful of items.

"Mary—what are you daydreaming about?" her mother demanded, breaking into Mary's thoughts after lunch as they began washing the dishes.

"Nothing at all, really," Mary lied, blushing.

"You barely said a word at lunch. I watched you," Constance said. "You hardly touched your soup."

"I wasn't hungry, I guess, Mother," Mary replied dreamily.

"Please stop gazing out into the garden and help me with the dishes," Constance ordered. "You see I have only one hand."

"Go rest, Mother," Mary insisted. "I will clean the dishes by myself."

After the dishes were washed and put away, Mary picked up a basket and headed out to the garden to pick vegetables for the evening meal.

The sun blazed down. Mary could see waves of heat rising off the near pasture.

As she bent to pull up some turnips, a movement at the back of the garden caught her eye. Jeremy was emerging, drenched with sweat, pulling out several heavy iron hoes and rakes.

On an impulse Mary dropped her vegetable basket to the dirt and hurried to the well at the side of the house.

A few seconds later she was standing in front of Jeremy, a tall pewter mug of cold well water in her hands. "Here," she said, thrusting the mug at him. "I thought you might be thirsty."

He smiled at her, breathing hard. His blond hair was matted flat to his forehead. He had removed his shirt, and his smooth, muscular chest glistened with sweat.

"You're very kind, Miss Fier," he said. He raised the mug to his lips and, keeping his blue eyes on her, thirstily gulped several mouthfuls. Then he tilted the mug over his head and dumped the rest on his hair. It poured over his hair and face and onto his tanned shoulders.

They both laughed.

"You may call me Mary," she told him shyly, feeling her cheeks redden. "You're a very hard worker," she added quickly.

Her remark seemed to please him. "I believe in doing a job well," he replied seriously. "My father and

I, we have always been poor. My father's health has never been good, so I have known hard work since I was barely out of swaddling clothes."

Mary gazed over his shoulder toward the rolling green pasture. "I work hard, too," she said wistfully. "There is so much to do on a farm this size."

"It is an admirable place," Jeremy said, turning to follow her gaze.

"It is very lonely here," Mary said suddenly. She hadn't planned on saying it. The words escaped before she could stop them. Her cheeks suddenly felt as if they were on fire. She lowered her eyes to the dirt.

"Do you have friends on other farms?" Jeremy asked softly. "Friends in town? Church friends?"

"No. I have my family. That is all," Mary said sadly. She cleared her throat. "But I have so many chores that I am usually too busy to think about friends and—"

"You're very pretty," Jeremy interrupted.

Startled by the compliment, Mary looked up to find his blue eyes staring intently at her.

"I like your hair," he said softly. "It is the color of sunset."

"Thank you, Jeremy," Mary replied awkwardly.

He took a step toward her, his eyes locked on hers.

What is he doing? Mary asked herself, feeling her heart start to pound.

Why is he staring at me like that? Is he trying to frighten me?

No. He's going to kiss me, Mary realized.

She started to take a step back, to move away. But she stopped.

He's going to kiss me. And I *want* him to.

"Mary!"

A voice behind her made her cry out.

She turned to see Rebecca running through the garden, waving to her wildly with both arms, her white apron flapping at the front of her dress as she ran.

Jeremy thrust the mug back at Mary, then turned and headed quickly toward the toolhouse.

"Rebecca, what is the matter?" Mary demanded, gripping the empty pewter mug in both hands.

"Have you seen Matthew? Edward? Where *are* they?" Rebecca cried, her features twisted in fear.

"Rebecca, what is the matter?" Mary repeated.

"Come quickly, Mary," Rebecca insisted, grabbing Mary's arm. "Please. Come. Something *horrible* has happened!"

Chapter
15

With Rebecca's shrill, frightened cry still ringing in her ears, Mary raced after her through the garden to the house.

"This way!" Rebecca shouted breathlessly, running through the kitchen and into the sitting room.

It took Mary's eyes a while to adjust to the sudden darkness. She gasped out loud when she saw Benjamin sprawled stiffly on his back on the floor.

"Look—that is how I found him!" Rebecca cried, pointing with a trembling finger. Her black hair had come undone and fell in disarray over her shoulders. Her dark lips formed an *O* of horror as she stared at the fallen man.

Mary dropped to her knees beside Benjamin. "Is he . . . is he . . . ?" she stammered. "Is he dead, Rebecca?"

She peered into Benjamin's face. His eyes were frozen in a glazed, wide-eyed stare. His mouth hung open loosely, revealing two rows of perfect teeth.

"I—I think so," Rebecca replied in a whisper. Then she ran back to the doorway, shouting, "Matthew! Matthew! Edward! Come quickly!"

Mary reached for Benjamin's hand and squeezed it. It was as cold as ice.

She swallowed hard, gaping down into the blank dark eyes that stared lifelessly up at her.

I've never seen a dead person, she thought.

"What's happening, Rebecca?" Edward had appeared in the doorway. "I heard you calling, and—" He lowered his eyes to the floor. "Father?"

"He—he must have been sitting there," Rebecca stammered, pointing to the high-backed chair against the wall. "He must have fallen. I think—"

"Father!" Edward cried again and dropped beside Mary. "Is he breathing?"

"I don't think so," Mary said softly. "I think—"

She and Edward both cried out at once as Benjamin blinked.

"Father!"

"Uncle Benjamin!"

He blinked again. His lips quivered. His mouth slowly closed.

"He's alive!" Mary told Rebecca happily. Rebecca let out a long sigh and closed her eyes. Slumping against a wall, she began whispering a prayer.

Benjamin raised his head groggily.

"Lie still, Father. Take your time," Edward urged, a hand on Benjamin's shoulder.

"I am able to rise," Benjamin insisted gruffly. "Let me up."

Edward moved his hands behind Benjamin's shoulders and helped him to sit up.

"Uncle Benjamin, what happened? How do you feel?" Mary asked.

"I must have been dozing," Benjamin growled, shaking his head, blinking several times to clear his eyes. "Fell from the chair, I guess."

Matthew burst into the room breathing hard, his round face bright red from the exertion of hurrying. "Was someone calling me?" he asked breathlessly. He cried out when he saw his brother on the floor.

"I am fine," Benjamin told him. "Do not get hysterical."

He started to climb to his feet, then hesitated. His expression turned to surprise.

"Uncle Benjamin, what is it?" Mary asked, still on her knees beside him. The others drew near.

"My left leg," Benjamin muttered. "I can't move it." He moved his right leg, drawing it up, then making the foot roll from side to side.

"I have no feeling," Benjamin said, sounding more startled than worried. "No feeling at all in the left leg."

Glancing up, Mary watched as her father grasped the odd three-toed medallion he wore around his neck. "How strange!" Matthew declared.

"Edward, help me to my feet," Benjamin ordered.

Edward obediently wrapped an arm around his father's shoulders and with great difficulty hoisted him to his feet.

Benjamin's eyes narrowed as he tried to put weight on his left leg. He would have fallen if Edward and Mary hadn't caught him.

"No feeling in the leg at all," Benjamin said thoughtfully. "It does not hurt. There is no pain. It does not feel like anything. It is as if the leg has been taken away from me."

Wisps of clouds floated low in a bright sky. The white trunks of the beech trees at the end of the pasture gleamed in the late afternoon sunlight.

Mary stepped along at the edge of the woods, lifting her skirt over low shrubs and rocks. Above her the leaves trembled in a soft breeze.

She turned where the trees ended and felt the blood pulse at her temples as Jeremy came into view. He was working shirtless as usual, his back to her, tugging with gloved hands at a tangle of brambles at his feet.

She crept closer. The tree leaves appeared to tremble harder.

Or is it my imagination? Mary wondered. Is it just my excitement?

For three days Jeremy had been working to clear the brambles from this new section of land. Each afternoon Mary had met him there. She brought him water from the well. Jeremy would take a break from his solitary efforts. They would sit together on a fallen tree trunk and talk.

Jeremy was so sweet, so understanding, so kind, Mary came to believe. She could feel herself growing close to him. She could feel herself beginning to fall in love with him. The feelings swept over her gently, almost like pulling on a favorite wool cloak.

Comfortable. Reassuring. Warm.

"I feel as if I've known you all my life," she told him after he had finished the mug of cold water. Her eyes trailed a gold and black butterfly as it fluttered near the trees.

Sitting beside her on the smooth tree trunk, he kicked the soft dirt with the heel of one boot. "Every afternoon I worry that you won't come," he said softly.

"Here I am," she replied, smiling.

"But if your father found out—" Jeremy started, staring into her eyes as if challenging her, a wave of blond hair tumbling over his forehead.

Mary's smile faded. "My father would not approve," she admitted. "After all, you are only a poor farmhand, without a shilling. And I—"

"You? You are royalty!" Jeremy joked. But there was bitterness behind the joke. "Queen Anne!" He rose to his feet and dipped his head in a courtly bow.

Mary giggled. "Please stop. I am sure that after time—"

"Time," Jeremy muttered. His eyes went to the thick brambles that rolled over the rocky ground. "Time for me to get back to work," he said. "Your father has instructed me to clear this field before the week is out."

"My father is not the true snob of the family," Mary said, lost in her own thoughts. "My uncle Benjamin would be much more alarmed than my father if he knew—"

"How does your uncle Benjamin feel?" Jeremy interrupted, his features tensing in concern.

"Not well," Mary replied, frowning. "His left arm has given out along with the leg."

"You mean—?"

"He cannot move the left arm now. He has no feeling in it. It is completely numb, he says. His entire left side is paralyzed."

"And how are his spirits?" Jeremy asked.

"Hard to tell," Mary replied thoughtfully. "He is as difficult and cantankerous as ever. He is not a man to give in to illness or affliction." She sighed. "Despite his strong spirit, he is as helpless as a baby."

"He is lucky to have you as a nurse," Jeremy replied, his eyes lighting up.

And before Mary could cry out or protest, he leaned over and pressed his mouth against hers.

Closing her eyes, Mary returned the kiss eagerly.

This is not proper. This isn't right.

But I do not care, she thought.

"Edward, please wait for me," Mary pleaded. "Don't walk so fast." Twigs snapped beneath her shoes as she hurried to catch up to him.

"Sorry," Edward said, turning to her. He pulled up a long, straight reed with his good hand and stuck one end in his mouth. "I was thinking about something."

Mary stepped up beside him breathlessly. "About your father?"

Edward nodded.

A bird cawed loudly above their heads. Mary gazed

up into a red sunset sky to see two large blackbirds standing side by side on a low limb.

"Are blackbirds good luck or bad?" she asked her cousin lightly.

"Bad luck, I believe," he replied thoughtfully. "Black is the color of death, is it not?"

"You do not have to be so gloomy," Mary complained. "I asked you to come out for a walk to cheer you up."

"Sorry." He frowned. "I am gloomy. I cannot help it, Mary."

"Because of your arm, Edward? It will heal."

"No," he replied, glancing down at the heavy sling. "I am worried about my father. And Rebecca. And—"

"Rebecca?" Mary interrupted, stepping over a tree stump. "Is Rebecca ill?"

Edward shook his head. "No. But she seems so weary all the time, so exhausted. So dispirited. She seems so different to me."

"I think she *is* tired," Mary told him. "Ezra is not an easy child."

Edward didn't reply. They continued their walk through the woods in silence. The last rays of sunlight slid between the slender trees, casting rippling blue shadows at their feet.

"It is nearly dinnertime," Edward said finally, chewing on the end of the reed. "Rebecca will worry."

"Let us head back," Mary agreed, running her fingers along the trunk of a tall oak as she turned around.

"I tried to speak to my father this afternoon," Edward told her, letting her take the lead. "I needed to speak to him about the receipts for the store. But he would only talk about his paralyzed arm and leg."

"Oh!"

They had walked into a swarm of buzzing gnats. Mary raised her hands to shield her eyes. She quickened her pace, nearly stumbling over a jagged white rock in her path.

"It is so strange about Father," Edward continued, still scratching his neck, even though the gnats had been left behind. "He feels perfectly fine. He seems to be in good health. He has no pain. And yet—"

"Perhaps his strength will return," Mary said hopefully. She stopped and turned to him. "You seem so troubled, Cousin. You can talk of nothing but our family's gloomy problems and mishaps."

"Everything was going so well for us," Edward replied with emotion. "We were all so happy. And now, all of a sudden—"

He stopped walking.

Mary saw his eyes grow wide and his mouth drop open. The reed fell to his feet.

"Edward—what is it?"

She turned as he pointed.

At first she thought the yellow glow was the sun poking between the trees.

But she quickly remembered that the sun was nearly down. This yellow glow was too bright, too fiery.

"Fire!" Edward screamed, the flames reflected in his frightened eyes. "The woods are on fire!"

"No!" Mary cried, grabbing his good arm. "Edward —look!"

Inside the glowing fireball a figure writhed.

"Someone is trapped in the flames!" Mary shrieked.

Chapter
16

"It cannot be!" Edward cried in a hoarse whisper. "It cannot be!"

But they both saw the dark figure of a girl clearly. The head rolled from side to side. Her arms were tied around a dark post behind her back that also burned with yellow fire.

Inside the flames.

Inside.

Being burned alive!

Gasping in horror, Mary began running toward the fire. Edward, struggling because his sling threw him off balance, followed behind.

"It is a girl!" Mary cried, raising both hands to her face. She stopped. She could feel the heat of the flames on her face.

Breathing hard, Edward stopped behind her.

Mary's breath caught in her throat. The fire seemed to grow hotter. Brighter.

She could see the girl clearly now inside the flames. Her mouth was open in a scream of agony. Flames climbed over her long curly hair. Flames shot up from her dark, old-fashioned-looking dress.

As the girl twisted in the flames, struggling against the stake behind her, she stared past Mary to Edward. Stared with wide, accusing eyes. Her entire body tossed with the fire. And through the flames her eyes burned into Edward's.

It took Mary a long time to realize that the terrified howl she heard behind her came from Edward.

She turned to see his entire body convulsed in a shudder of terror. Edward's dark eyes bulged in disbelief. The hot yellow firelight cast an eerie glow over his trembling body.

"Susannah!" Edward cried, recognizing at last the girl in the fire. "Susannah Goode!"

As he cried out her name, the vision darkened and disappeared. The burning girl vanished.

The woods were dark and silent—except for Edward's horrified howl.

"I have had nightmares about the fire for the past two nights," Mary told Jeremy. "When I close my eyes, I see that poor girl, her hands tied behind her, her hair in flames, her entire body in flames. It was two days ago, Jeremy, but I still . . . I . . . I . . ."

Mary's voice broke. She leaned her head against Jeremy's solid shoulder.

They were seated close together on a low mound of

straw in the corner of the new field. Ahead of them, at the tree line, she could see the brambles and tree branches Jeremy had cleared from the field that morning.

The late afternoon sky was gray and overcast. Occasional drops of cold rain indicated a storm was approaching.

"Sometimes the light plays tricks in the trees," Jeremy suggested, speaking softly, soothingly, his arm gently around Mary's trembling shoulders. "Sometimes you see a bright glowing reflection, and it's only the sun against a mulberry bush."

"This was not a bush," Mary replied edgily. "It could not have been a bush."

"Sometimes the trees cast strange shadows," Jeremy insisted.

"Jeremy!" Mary rose angrily to her feet. "Edward recognized the girl! It could not have been a shadow! He *recognized* her!"

Jeremy patted the straw, urging her to sit down. "I am sorry," he said softly. "How does your cousin feel? Has he recovered?"

"Edward has become very quiet," Mary told him, dropping back onto the straw but keeping her distance from Jeremy. "He will not talk about what we saw. He will not talk about much at all. He seems very far away. I—I think he has nightmares, too."

Jeremy gazed at her but didn't reply.

"I am sorry to burden you with my troubles," Mary said, frowning. She gripped the basket she had carried with her from the house. "I had better be going and let you get back to work."

She could see the hurt in his eyes. "I want you to share your troubles with me," he said. "You do not burden me, Mary." He lowered his eyes to the basket. "What is in there?"

"Sweet rolls," she replied. "I baked them this morning for Rebecca. I'm going to take them to her now. Rebecca has been in such low spirits lately. I thought to cheer her."

He gazed at her with pleading eyes. A smile slowly formed on his lips as he pressed his hands together in a prayerful position.

"Do not beg," Mary scolded, chuckling. "You may have one." She reached into the basket and pulled out a large sweet roll.

"I would rather have this," Jeremy said, grinning, and he sprang forward and began kissing her.

The sweet roll fell out of her hand into the straw. Mary made no move to retrieve it. Instead, she placed her hand behind Jeremy's neck and held him close.

When the kiss ended, she jumped to her feet, brushing the straw off the long white apron she wore over her dress. She adjusted the comb that held her hair and gazed up at the sky.

Dark storm clouds rolled over the gray sky.

"I had better go on to Edward's house," she said.

"Have you told your father?" Jeremy demanded, picking up the sweet roll from the straw and examining it. "Have you told him about us? About how we feel?"

Mary frowned. "No. It is not the right time, Jeremy. Father is so terribly troubled."

"You told your father about the fire? About the girl burning in the flames?"

"Yes." Mary nodded solemnly, her skin very pale in the approaching darkness. "I told him about what Edward and I saw. He had the strangest reaction."

"Strange?"

"He wears a silver disk around his neck. He always wears it. It was given to him in the Old Country by his grandmother. It is jeweled and has tiny silver claws. Well, when I told Father about the girl in the fire, he cried out as if he had been stabbed—and grabbed the disk tightly in one hand."

"And what did he say to you, Mary?" Jeremy asked quietly, carefully picking straw off the sticky roll.

Mary's face darkened as the storm clouds lowered. "That is the strangest part," she whispered. "He didn't say anything. Not a word. He just stood there gripping the silver disk, staring out the window. He didn't say a word."

"That is very strange," Jeremy replied, lowering the sweet roll, a thoughtful expression on his face.

"I must leave now," Mary told him sadly. "Before the storm." She lifted the basket and straightened the linen cover over the sweet rolls.

She took a few steps toward the pasture, then suddenly stopped and turned back to Jeremy. Still seated in the mound of straw, he gazed up at her, chewing a mouthful of the roll.

"What of *your* father?" Mary demanded. "Have you spoken to him about me?"

The question appeared to startle Jeremy. He choked for a moment on the roll, then swallowed hard.

"I would like to meet your father," Mary told him playfully. "I would very much like to see your house and meet your father."

Jeremy climbed to his feet, his forehead knitted in concern. "I am afraid that is not a good idea," he told her, avoiding her eyes. "My father is . . . quite ill. He is not strong enough to welcome company."

Mary could not conceal her disappointment. "I guess we are doomed to meet in the woods for the rest of our lives," she said with a sigh.

Edward's house was a small one-story structure, built of the stones that had been cleared from the crop fields and pasture. It had a sloping slate roof and two small windows in the front.

The house sat at the edge of the woods. From the front, one could gaze across the pasture to Benjamin and Matthew's house on the other side.

As Mary made her way from the back field where Jeremy worked, she felt the first large drops of rain start to fall. She thought about her father as she hurried on.

I wish I could tell him about Jeremy, she thought sadly. But he is in no mood for more troubling news.

Her thoughts turned to her ailing uncle Benjamin. The poor man had awakened them all, screaming at the top of his lungs in the middle of the night.

Mary had reached his room first, followed by her frantic father and mother. At first they thought Benjamin was suffering a nightmare. But his screams were not because of a dream.

During the night, he had lost the use of his right leg.

Mary's uncle could now move only his head and right arm.

Matthew was becoming more and more distant and aloof, lost in his own thoughts. Her cousin, Edward, had become glum and silent. And Rebecca—Rebecca appeared wearier and older, as if she were aging a year every day.

Mary gripped the basket of sweet rolls tightly in one hand and approached Edward's house. "Rebecca?" she called.

No reply.

"Rebecca? It is I, Mary."

Still no reply.

The storm clouds gathered overhead. Raindrops pattered against the hard ground.

Mary knocked on the front door.

It is so strangely quiet, she thought, shifting the weight of the basket. I can always hear Ezra's shouts and cries when I approach this house. Why do I not hear him now?

She knocked again.

Receiving no response, she pushed open the door and entered.

"Rebecca? Ezra?"

The front room was surprisingly bright. The candles on the wall were lighted, as were candles on a small oak table beside the hearth. A low fire crackled under a pot in the hearth.

"Rebecca?"

Where can she be? Mary wondered.

"Rebecca? Are you home?"

As she set the basket down on the floor, Mary heard

a soft creaking sound. She listened for a few seconds, trying to figure out what was making the sound.

Then she suddenly noticed the black shadow swinging back and forth across the floor.

Confused, she stared down at the slowly moving shadow for a long while, following it with her eyes narrowed.

Creak. Creak.

The odd sound repeated in rhythm with the shadow.

Then she raised her eyes and saw what was casting the shadow—and started to scream.

Chapter
17

"Rebecca!" Mary managed to choke out. Rebecca's body swung heavily above Mary's head.

Gaping up in horror, Mary saw the heavy rope tied around Rebecca's neck and suspended from the rafter.

She saw Rebecca's arms dangling lifelessly.

She saw Rebecca's face, the skin dark, the eyes bulging.

Creak. Creak.

"Rebecca! Nooooooooooooo!" Mary uttered a high-pitched wail and dropped to her knees. The floor tilted up to meet her. She felt ready to faint.

She shut her eyes and shook her head, as if trying to shake the whole scene away.

But even with her eyes closed, Mary saw Rebecca's body swinging from the rope like a heavy, ripe fruit.

What happened here?
Did Rebecca hang herself?
Was she murdered?

The horrifying questions forced their way into Mary's mind.

She opened her eyes and saw Rebecca's dress hovering beside her face.

"I—I cannot accept this," Mary said. "I—I—cannot—" She began to vomit then, her entire body convulsing in tremor after tremor.

Until she was crying. And screaming.

And on her feet again.

And outside. Without realizing it, she had started to run.

In the now heavy rain. The cold rainwater washing her face, drenching her hair, soaking through her dress.

Her shoes splashing up puddles as she ran through the soft dirt toward her home.

"Edward! Where are you? Edward?"

And where is Ezra? she wondered.

And how will I tell everyone?

And how will I ever get the hideous sight out of my mind?

How? How? How?

The pouring rain couldn't wash away the image of Rebecca, her head twisted at such a strange angle, swinging so gently from the ceiling.

The rain couldn't wash away the blackened skin, the bulging eyes.

The rain couldn't drown out the *creak-creak* of the body as it swung gently back and forth.

"Edward! Father! Mother! Help me!"

Mary ran through the rain, her arms outstretched as if reaching for help. Ran screaming without hearing her own cries.

Rebecca, you cannot be dead.

Please do not be dead!

Do not be dead, Rebecca.

Mary was halfway across the pasture now, slipping over the puddled grass. Rainwater matted her hair against her head, ran down her forehead, and blurred her vision.

The house loomed ahead of her, gray against the low black sky.

"Edward! Where are you? Edward? Father? Father?"

Her feet slid out from under her, and she fell, sprawling facedown in the soft cold mud. She landed hard on her elbows and knees.

"Oh!"

Maybe I will not get up. Maybe I shall stay here forever.

Maybe I shall just lie here in the mud and let the rain carry me away, float me away from—everything.

With a desperate cry she pulled herself to her feet, her clothes covered with mud, her hair hanging heavily in her face.

She took a few steps, then stopped with a shocked gasp.

Who is that?

A stranger standing in the middle of the pasture.

Dressed in black, standing as still as death.

Am I seeing things?

She pushed her hair out of her eyes with both hands and wiped the rainwater from her face.

No.

He was still there.

Who can it be?

Why is he standing so still in the pouring rain and staring at me?

She called out to him.

The dark figure stared at her without moving.

Chapter
18

Mary called again.

Beyond the pasture the trees shivered and were bent low in a howling gust of wind.

The man didn't move.

Trembling from the cold, from the horror, Mary took a reluctant step toward him. Then another.

The wind picked up and swirled around her. The rain swept over her like cold ocean waves.

Her shoes sank into the mud as she made her way closer.

He was standing so still, Mary saw, squinting through the heavy curtain of rain.

As still as a statue.

A statue?

It is a scarecrow, she realized.

Of course. That is why it doesn't move.

A scarecrow.

As she ventured closer, she saw rainwater rolling off the brim of its black hat, saw the dark sleeves of its long coat flutter in the sweeping winds.

Who put a scarecrow here? Mary wondered.

Then her next thought made her stop short: Why would anyone stand a scarecrow in the middle of a grassy pasture?

She shielded her eyes with one hand and squinted hard.

And took another step closer. Then another.

Finally through the heavy downpour she recognized the face under the wide-brimmed black hat.

"Uncle Benjamin!"

Once again Mary stared into the blank-eyed face of death.

Benjamin Fier was the scarecrow.

His body was propped up nearly as straight as if he were standing. His arms hung lifelessly at his sides.

His face was bright purple. His hair spilled out from the hat and lay matted against his head.

He gaped at Mary with blank eyes, deathly white eyes, the pupils rolled up into his head.

"Uncle Benjamin!"

The wind gusted hard, shaking the body, making the limp arms swing back and forth.

The body turned again. Benjamin's mouth dropped open, as if he wanted to speak. But the only sound Mary could hear was the heavy groan of the wind.

Mary's body convulsed in a cold shudder of horror. She spun away from the ghastly sight, the dark grass tilting and swirling wildly around her. Her stomach heaved, but there was nothing left to vomit.

Rebecca. Benjamin. Both dead.

Dead. Dead. Dead.

The word repeated in her mind, pounded into her thoughts, pounded against her brain like the cold rain.

The cold, cold rain that poured off her uncle's hat. Cold as death.

Is everyone dead?

Has my whole family been killed?

Mary stared toward the house. It seemed so distant now. So dark and distant. Far away, on the other side of the storm.

Has everyone been killed? Mary wondered.

Everyone?

And then: *Will I be next?*

Chapter
19

The funeral for Rebecca and Benjamin was held two days later. The rain had stopped the day before, but the sky remained gray and overcast.

The graves had been dug in a corner of the field Jeremy had been working to clear. White rocks had been placed at their heads since there were no gravestone carvers in the village.

Standing at the side of the open graves as the minister delivered his funeral speech, Mary gazed at the dark-suited mourners.

Several people had come from the village and neighboring farms to attend. Their blank faces and hushed whispers revealed more curiosity than sadness.

Mary glanced at them quickly, then turned her attention to the members of her family. As she studied them one by one, the minister's droning voice faded into the background.

The past two days had been a waking nightmare in the stone farmhouse that had so recently rung with laughter. Now the faces of her family, Mary saw, were pale and drawn, eyes red-rimmed and brimming with tears, mouths drawn tight, in straight lines of sadness —and fear.

On the far side of the graves Edward Fier stood with his shoulders hunched, his head bowed. His hands were clasped tightly in front of him.

At first Edward had reacted to the deaths of his wife and father with stunned disbelief. In a frenzy he had shaken Mary violently by the shoulders, demanding that she stop telling such wild tales, refusing to believe her gruesome descriptions.

But her racking sobs forced Edward to see that Mary hadn't been dreaming. With a wild cry he had burst from the house, out into the driving rain, running awkwardly with his sling bobbing in front of him, running to see the horrors for himself.

Afterward, Edward had become silent, barely speaking a word. He spent a day in silent prayer. When he emerged, his eyes were dull and blank.

Edward wandered silently around the house like a living corpse. Constance, crying without stop, was forced to tend to Ezra. Matthew made the funeral arrangements and supervised the digging of the graves since Edward was unable to speak to anyone.

Ezra sensed immediately that something terrible had happened. He had to be told that his mother was never coming back.

It had fallen to Constance to tell the boy. Mary watched from a corner of the room, huddled next to the hearth.

Constance had drawn Ezra onto her lap and, tears running down her cheeks, told him that his mother had gone to heaven.

"Can I go, too?" Ezra had asked innocently.

Constance tried to hold herself in, but the boy's words caused her to sob more, and Mary had to carry him away.

Afterward, Ezra had acted troubled. He stayed underfoot while the funerals were being planned and cried loudly if anyone spoke a harsh word in the house.

Poor Ezra, Mary thought, gazing at the boy, so tiny and solemn in his black coat and breeches. Ezra's black hat was several sizes too big for him and fell down over his ears.

The minister droned on. Mary turned her gaze to her father. Matthew stood beside her, his large stomach heaving with each breath he took, his eyes narrowed, staring straight ahead.

He had reacted more strangely than anyone when he heard the news of the two murders. Mary had expected him to crumple with grief, especially at the news of the loss of his brother.

But Matthew had only reacted in fear. His eyes had narrowed. He had glanced nervously around the sitting room as if expecting to see someone who didn't belong there.

Then, gripping the three-toed amulet at his throat, he had disappeared from the room.

Late that night, while the house was cloaked in silent sadness, Mary had spied Matthew in his room, seated at his worktable, his face deep in shadow. Holding the strange medallion in front of him with both hands, Matthew was repeating its words aloud, again and again like a chant: *"Dominatio per malum."*

Mary wondered what the words meant.

Was it some kind of prayer?

She didn't know any Latin.

The next day Matthew had still seemed more frightened than sad. His eyes kept searching the farm, as if he expected an unwanted visitor.

Mary was desperate to talk to him about what had happened. But he avoided her each time she approached. She was forced to spend most of her time trying to comfort her mother.

The minister continued his prayers. One after the other the two pine coffins were lowered into the graves.

Mary suddenly saw Jeremy standing at the edge of the crowd of villagers. He was dressed in black breeches and a loose-fitting black shirt. He was wearing a battered old hat with a broken brim.

Despite her grief, a faint smile crossed her face. She had never seen Jeremy in a hat before.

Mary hadn't seen Jeremy in two days. Nearly all work had stopped on the farm, and Jeremy had been sent home.

She was surprised to see him now. Their eyes met. She stared at him, wondering what he was thinking.

He lowered his eyes, his expression troubled.

After the graves were covered over, the minister and

villagers departed quickly. Constance and Matthew led Ezra back to the house. Edward remained standing stiffly, staring down at the graves.

Mary saw Jeremy walking slowly in the direction of the toolhouse behind the garden. Taking a deep breath, she decided to follow him.

"Jeremy—wait!"

She caught up with him at the side of the toolhouse and threw herself into his arms. "Jeremy. Oh, Jeremy. I—I have missed you. I need you. I really do!"

Grabbing both of his hands, she tugged him behind the toolhouse, out of view of the house, and breathlessly kissed him, pulling his head to hers.

To Mary's surprise, Jeremy resisted. He gently pushed her away.

"Jeremy—it has been so horrible!" Mary cried. "The past two days. A nightmare. I—"

She stopped when she saw the troubled expression on his face. She reached for him again, but he took a step back.

"Jeremy—what is wrong?" Mary demanded, suddenly frightened. "What has happened? Why are you looking at me like that?"

He locked his eyes on hers. "Mary, I have to tell you something," he said in a low, trembling voice.

Mary started to answer, but her voice caught in her throat. She searched his eyes, trying to find a clue in their blue depths.

"Jeremy . . . I . . ."

"Please. Let me talk," he said sharply. "This is hard. This is very hard."

"What?" she managed to whisper.

"I—I know who killed Rebecca and Benjamin," Jeremy told her.

A cold chill ran down Mary's back, a chill of fear. And heavy dread.

"Who?" she asked.

Chapter
20

Jeremy lowered himself to a sitting position on the ground and pulled Mary down beside him. They sat with their backs against the wall. Jeremy gripped her hand tightly.

"I prayed this would not happen," he told her. He tore off his ill-fitting hat and tossed it away.

"What, Jeremy?" Mary demanded. "Who killed Rebecca and Benjamin?"

Jeremy's eyes were tense as he raised them to hers. "My father," he told her. "My father killed them both."

Mary gasped and pulled her hand away. "I—I do not understand." She started to get to her feet, but Jeremy pulled her back down.

"I will explain," he said. "Please. Let me explain."

"You told me your father was ill!" Mary cried

angrily. "You told me he was too weak to have visitors. And now you say—"

"My father is an evil man," Jeremy admitted, burrowing his hands into the dirt beside him. "But there is a reason. He had much evil done to him."

"I—I do not understand a word you're saying!" Mary declared.

"I will explain it all, Mary," he replied quietly. "You shall hear it all. The whole unhappy story. Just as my father told it to me. For I was born after it all happened."

Mary sighed and pressed her back against the toolhouse wall. She clasped her hands tightly in her lap and listened with growing horror to Jeremy's story.

"My father's name is William Goode," he began. "I told you my name was Thorne because I needed work, and my father instructed me that your father would never hire a Goode."

"So you lied to me?" Mary asked sharply. "You gave a false name on the day we met?"

"It was the only lie I ever told you," Jeremy replied softly. "It was a lie I regret. Please believe me. My name is Jeremy Goode. I was born after my father left a village known as Wickham in Massachusetts Bay Colony."

"My family also comes from Wickham!" Mary cried with surprise.

"I know," Jeremy said darkly. He tossed a handful of dirt past his shoes. "I have a brother. George. Two years ago he chose to return to Wickham. He could no longer tolerate my father's insane obsession."

"Obsession?" Mary asked, bewildered.

"Let me go back farther in time, Mary. You will soon understand. Although you will wish you did not."

Jeremy took a deep breath and continued. "When my father lived in Wickham, he had a wife named Martha and a daughter named Susannah," he told her, staring straight ahead. "He had a life, a happy life. But your father and your uncle robbed him of that life. They robbed him and the entire town."

Mary swallowed hard, then gazed at Jeremy in bewilderment. "How can that be?"

"Your uncle Benjamin was magistrate. His brother Matthew was his assistant. Benjamin accused Martha and Susannah of practicing the dark arts. He put them on trial. He burned them at the stake as witches."

"Susannah Goode!" Mary cried, raising her hands to her face. "That is the name Edward cried when we saw the girl burning in the woods!"

"Benjamin burned Susannah as a witch to keep her from marrying your cousin, Edward!"

"No!" Mary exclaimed, shaking her head as if trying to shake away Jeremy's words. "No! Stop!"

"I cannot stop until my story is finished," Jeremy said heatedly.

"But Edward is the most pious man I know!" Mary declared. "Edward would never allow his father to burn an innocent girl!"

"Edward did allow it," Jeremy replied in a low whisper. "He did nothing to save Susannah or her mother. Edward trusted his father. He did not know the villainy that Benjamin Fier was capable of."

"But—" Mary's voice caught in her throat.

"Your father, Matthew Fier, was also a villain. He promised to save Martha and Susannah. He took money from my father in exchange for saving their lives. He robbed my father. Then Benjamin and Matthew robbed the village and fled. And Martha and Susannah, an innocent woman and girl, burned at the stake."

"No!" Mary uttered in a hoarse whisper. "I cannot believe this, Jeremy."

"This is the story my father has told me all my life," Jeremy said, grabbing her hand. "All my life he has sought revenge against your family, against the Fiers. And now . . . now my father has begun to take his revenge. He has murdered two Fiers. He will murder you all—unless we do something."

Mary stared into the gray sky as if in a daze. She didn't move or speak.

Jeremy's words hung in her mind, lingered, repeated, creating ugly pictures, pictures of fire and suffering and treachery.

"Why should I believe you?" she demanded finally, her voice small and frightened. "Why should I believe these horrible accusations you make about my father and uncle?"

Jeremy's reply stunned her. "Because I love you," he said.

She gasped.

"I love you, too, Jeremy," she replied breathlessly.

He wrapped his arms around her and pulled her close. They held the embrace for a long time, her face pressed against his, their arms around each other, not moving, barely breathing.

When he finally pulled away, Jeremy stared at her intently. "We can stop the hatred now, Mary," he said softly. "You and I. We can stop the hatred between our families so that no one else will die."

"How, Jeremy?" she asked, holding on to him. "How can we?"

"We love each other," Jeremy said with emotion. "We will marry. When we marry, our families will be one. The old hatred will be forgotten. And the Goodes and the Fiers will live in peace."

"Yes!" Mary cried.

As they kissed, they didn't see the dark-coated person move silently away from the side of the toolhouse.

Wrapped in each other's arms, they didn't realize that this figure had been so near the entire time, had heard their conversation, had listened in shock and dismay to Jeremy's story.

Edward Fier took a deep breath, then another, trying to calm his pounding heart.

After the funeral he had followed Mary, planning to ask her to look after Ezra. To his surprise, he had spied her with Jeremy. Leaning against the side of the toolhouse, Edward had eavesdropped, clinging to every word with growing horror.

Now Edward's horror mixed with anger as he strode quickly to his uncle Matthew's house.

"Lies!" he declared to himself. "The boy speaks lies. And he has filled poor Mary's head with these unthinkable false tales!"

My father did not accuse Susannah Goode unjustly, Edward told himself. My father was a righteous man. Susannah burned because she was truly a follower of the Evil One.

Halfway to the house Edward stopped short.

The fire he and Mary had seen in the woods flashed into his mind as brightly as if he were seeing it again. And inside the fire was Susannah Goode, twisting in agony, screaming in pain.

"No!" Edward cried. He closed his eyes to erase the image. "Susannah burned because she deserved to burn! My father and uncle are righteous men!"

His heart racing, he burst into the house. Ezra and Constance were in the front room. "Edward," Constance started, "come sit down and—"

"Not now," Edward said brusquely.

Her mouth dropped open in surprise.

"Hello, Papa!" Ezra called.

His mind blazing, Edward ignored the child. He rushed past them both, heading for Matthew's room.

A fire crackled in Matthew's fireplace despite the heat of the afternoon. Edward pushed open the door without knocking. "Uncle Matthew?" he called breathlessly.

Matthew was seated at his worktable, papers strewn messily across the top. Still in his mourning coat, he appeared to be gazing into the fire.

He turned in surprise as Edward burst into the room. "Edward—the funeral. It went well, I suppose. I—"

"Uncle Matthew, I must ask you something!" Edward cried, his dark eyes burning into his uncle's. "I heard a horrifying story just now, about you and my father. About the days when we lived in Wickham."

Matthew's lips twitched. His eyes widened in surprise. "What kind of story, Nephew?"

"About Susannah Goode," Edward blurted out. "That she was falsely accused. That she was condemned to burn by my father even though he knew of her innocence. That you and my father robbed the town and fled."

Leaning over his table, Matthew Fier closed his eyes and rubbed the lids with his thumbs.

"These stories cannot be true!" Edward declared breathlessly. "Tell me that they are lies, Uncle. Tell me!"

Matthew slowly opened his eyes and trained them on Edward. "Calm yourself, Edward," he urged softly. "Rest easy, my boy. Of course those stories are lies. There isn't a word of truth in them."

Chapter
21

"All lies," Matthew repeated, staring hard into the fire. He rose from his chair and turned to Edward. "I must know who is spreading these false stories."

Edward hesitated.

To his surprise, he saw that Matthew's entire body was trembling.

The door burst open and Mary entered, her face flushed, her expression troubled. "Father, I must speak to you. I—"

Seeing his daughter, Matthew fell back into his chair. Uttering a low, mournful sigh, he covered his face with his hands. "Mary, poor Mary," he muttered to himself. "Will he kill you, too, before this is over?"

"Father, what are you saying?" Mary demanded, still in the doorway.

Matthew remained with his face hidden behind his hands. When he finally looked up, he had tears in his eyes.

"Edward," he said in a whisper, "the stories are true."

Edward cried out in shock. "No, Uncle Matthew! Please—do not tell me this!"

"I must!" Matthew choked out. "I must. I cannot carry on with my lies. Seeing Mary made me realize it is time to finally tell the truth. We are all in too much danger."

Mary took a few steps into the room. "What are you saying?" she demanded of her father. She turned to Edward. "Cousin, what are you talking about?"

Edward stared at her in stunned silence. "An innocent girl—a girl I loved—died because of my father." He gave a pained sob. "And I condemned her as much as my father did!"

Slumped at the table, Matthew suddenly looked very old. His jowls sagged. All the life seemed to drain from his eyes. "Your father wanted the best for you, Edward."

"The best?" Edward cried bitterly. "You never told me why we left Wickham. My father never gave me a choice!"

"Yes," Matthew insisted, avoiding Edward's accusing stare. "He and I both wanted to make sure you never experienced the poverty we experienced. But we went too far."

"You overheard my talk with Jeremy," Mary accused Edward.

Edward nodded. "Yes. And I came directly here. To confront your father. To learn——"

"The stories are all true?" Mary cried shrilly, raising her hands to her cheeks.

"I am afraid they are," her father confessed sadly.

"Poor Susannah Goode. How I wronged her," Edward said, swallowing hard.

"You and Uncle Benjamin burned an innocent woman and girl?" Mary demanded, her eyes burning into her father's.

Matthew turned away. "It was a long time ago. Before you were born," he told Mary weakly.

"And now William Goode has had his revenge," Edward said in a trembling, low voice. "He has murdered my wife and my father."

Matthew rose to his feet, his face bright red, his hands shaking. "We will make him pay!" he shouted angrily.

"No!" Edward and Mary shouted in unison.

"We are even now!" Edward cried passionately. "We will make peace with the Goodes."

"Peace?" Matthew protested heatedly. "Peace? Edward, have you lost your senses? He *murdered* Rebecca and Benjamin!"

"We will make peace," Edward insisted, narrowing his eyes at his uncle, his features set in firm determination.

"Jeremy Goode and I are in love," Mary blurted out.

"The farmhand?" Matthew cried. "The farmhand is a Goode?"

"Jeremy is William's son," Mary told him. "And we wish to marry."

"No! Never!" Matthew declared, pounding his fist on the table, sending papers flying to the floor.

"Yes!" Edward insisted. "Yes, they *will* marry. The wound between our families will be healed. And you, Uncle, will offer your apology to William Goode and his son."

Matthew glared at them both. Then his gaze softened. He sighed wearily and shrugged under the heavy black mourning coat. "I will never apologize to a murderer," he muttered.

"You and Benjamin are also murderers!" Mary cried.

Her words stung Matthew. He closed his eyes. He was silent for a long while.

"Well, Father?" Mary demanded.

"We will heal the wounds," Matthew replied finally. "I will apologize as you wish. You may marry William Goode's son if you so desire."

"I do so desire," Mary replied quickly.

"This murderous feud will be ended," Edward said solemnly. "The two families will no longer be enemies."

"Yes," Matthew agreed. "When a week of mourning has passed, invite them both—William and Jeremy— to dinner. At that time I will do what is necessary, I promise you both, to end this bitter feud forever."

"Thank you, Father!" Mary cried happily.

"Thank you, Uncle," Edward declared.

"It will be done," Matthew said softly.

* * *

The week of mourning passed slowly for Mary. Sadness hovered low over the house and farm.

Mary did her household chores and helped Constance care for Ezra. Ezra kept asking when his mother would return. He didn't seem able or willing to understand that she was never coming back.

Edward remained at his house, buried in thoughts of the past, awash in regret, reliving the painful memories as if they had happened the day before instead of eighteen years earlier.

Matthew made an effort to do his work. But he seldom spoke to anyone in the house. His eyes remained empty, cold, focused far away.

Dinners were eaten in uncomfortable silence. Mary found herself thinking of Jeremy.

This sadness that covers the house like a dark curtain will lift when Jeremy and I are together, when Matthew makes his apology to William, and the two families are as one, she thought.

And finally the evening arrived, a cool, clear evening with a hint of autumn in the air. Inside the house the tangy aroma of a roasting goose floated through the rooms. Candles in a silver candelabra glowed in the center of the dining room table, which Mary and Constance had carefully laid out with the family's best dishes and serving utensils.

Mary sat, tensed, waiting for Jeremy and his father to arrive. Ezra tried to climb on Edward, but Edward impatiently pushed him off.

Hands clasped behind his back, Matthew paced the floor, frowning. Constance remained in the kitchen, tending to the goose.

Everyone in the family is so nervous and silent, Mary thought. And I am the most nervous of all.

How difficult it will be for Father to see William Goode after all these years. How difficult for them both.

But how fortunate that Jeremy and I will be able to bring them together, to end the years of hatred.

What a tragedy that Rebecca and Benjamin had to die before this horrid feud could end, Mary thought sadly.

A loud knock on the door jarred Mary from her thoughts.

She jumped to her feet and hurried across the room.

"Hello, Jeremy!" she cried, pulling open the door. She gazed over his shoulder. "Where is your father?"

Wearing a loose-fitting white wool shirt that was tied at the waist over black breeches, Jeremy stepped into the room, a fixed smile on his face. "Good evening, Mary," he returned her greeting quietly but did not answer her question.

This is so wonderful, Mary thought, gazing at him. *This is a dream come true.*

Jeremy is here—in my house! I'm so happy!

Mary couldn't know that in two seconds' time— two ticks of the clock—her happiness would turn into unspeakable horror.

Chapter
22

As Jeremy crossed the room to greet him, Matthew Fier raised the silver disk over his head and pointed it at Jeremy.

Jeremy hesitated. His smile faded.

Matthew called out the words on the back of the disk: *"Dominatio per malum!"*

Jeremy's head exploded with a low *pop!*

At first no one was certain where the sound had come from.

Mary was the first to realize that something horrible had happened.

Jeremy's skull cracked open, and the skin on his face blistered and peeled away. Pink brains bubbled up from his open skull. His face appeared to melt away, and another face pushed up from under the shattered skull.

Another head appeared on Jeremy's body.

The head of a white-haired man, his cheeks scarlet, his eyes brimming with hatred.

"William Goode!" Matthew declared, still holding the strange medallion above his head.

"Yes, it is I," William replied weakly. "I almost stole your daughter from you, Matthew. But your powers are stronger than mine."

"Jeremy!" Mary shrieked, finally finding her voice. "Jeremy! Jeremy! Where is my Jeremy?"

"There *is* no Jeremy!" her father told her. "There *never was* a Jeremy, Daughter! It was William Goode all along! He used his powers to make himself appear young!"

William Goode glared across the candle-lit room at Matthew, his hatred too strong for words. He raised a trembling hand to point an accusing finger at Matthew.

"Jeremy!" Mary cried, her eyes darting frantically from face to face. "Jeremy! Where are you? Where is my Jeremy? Where have you hid him?"

"Constance—help comfort Mary!" Matthew ordered.

But Constance remained rigid with terror against the wall.

With an animal cry of rage Matthew again pointed the amulet at the figure of William Goode. *"Dominatio per malum!"* he screamed. *"Power through evil!"*

William's entire body trembled. His eyes rolled up in his head. The skin on his face began to crumble.

He sank to his knees. His clothing appeared to fold over him as he crumbled, crumbled in seconds to powdery gray dust.

"Jeremy!" Mary shrieked, racing back and forth across the room, her eyes wide and fearful. "Jeremy—where is my Jeremy?"

As Matthew stared down at the pile of dust under the crumpled clothing, a triumphant smile crossed his face. He tossed back his head, opened his mouth wide, and began to laugh.

A loud, gleeful laugh.

"Jeremy? Where is Jeremy?" Mary demanded.

"Where did the man go?" Ezra asked Edward.

His eyes wide with horror, Edward grabbed Ezra up into his arms and held him pressed tight against his chest.

Matthew laughed harder, joyful tears pouring down his face.

"Stop laughing, Matthew!" Constance screamed, running over to him. "Stop it!"

Matthew laughed even harder.

"Where is Jeremy? Where is he hiding?" Mary cried.

Holding Ezra over his shoulder, Edward grabbed Mary's hand. "Come on," he urged her firmly.

"What? I cannot go without Jeremy," Mary replied, gazing at Edward with dazed, unseeing eyes.

"Come on, Mary." Edward tugged her hand. "We have to leave. We have to get *out* of here!"

Holding his bulging sides, Matthew roared with laughter.

"Stop laughing—please, Matthew!" his wife pleaded.

Matthew laughed harder.

Constance began pounding her fists on his chest. "Stop laughing! Stop laughing! Matthew—can you not stop?"

"Mary—come on!" Edward pulled Mary to the door.

Ezra, clinging to his father's shoulder, began to cry.

Edward pulled Mary out the door into the cool night.

"Jeremy? Is Jeremy coming with us?" Mary demanded.

"No," Edward told her. "Come with me. We have to leave this farm. Tonight." He pulled her into the darkness.

In the house Constance continued to plead with her husband. "Matthew—stop laughing! Stop! Can you stop? Can you stop now?"

Despite his wife's desperate pleas, Matthew continued to laugh.

His round face bright scarlet, his enormous stomach heaving, his mouth gaping open, he laughed and laughed.

Loud, helpless laughter.

Maddened by his triumph, Matthew would laugh without stop for the rest of his life.

PART THREE

Western Pennsylvania Wilderness
1725

Chapter
23

Ezra Fier dug his bootheels into the horse's sides and urged the old mare on. Low branches and shrubs brushed against his worn leather breeches. Ezra kept his eyes straight ahead.

Twenty-one now, a slender young man, Ezra had his mother's straight black hair and broad forehead and his father's thoughtful eyes.

As he rode through the thick brush, Ezra thought of his father and his aunt Mary, and his bitterness grew.

My poor father, he tried so hard to keep us alive in this lonely wilderness. He worked so hard to keep a roof over our heads and food in our mouths.

But he was never the same after that strange night, my last night at Great-Uncle Matthew's farm.

Ezra remembered that night as one might view a faded photograph. He could picture the young man

Jeremy Goode. Something bad had happened to Jeremy Goode. Aunt Mary had started to scream. Great-Uncle Matthew had started to laugh crazily.

And then Edward—Ezra's father—had pulled Ezra away, pulled him into the night, away from the farm, along with Aunt Mary.

Ezra had been only six. But the frightening memories of that night haunted him still.

As he rode through the thick woods to his Great-Uncle Matthew's farm, the bitterness of the past fifteen years washed over him, blanketing him in darkness despite the dappled gold of the bright sun filtering through the trees.

Edward had died of exhaustion, still a young man. Ezra's Aunt Mary had never recovered her senses. She would go for weeks without speaking, then suddenly declare, "I am a witch! I am a witch!"

Often Mary would stare out into the trees for hours on end. "Is Jeremy coming?" she would ask in a pitiful small voice. "Is Jeremy coming soon?"

Ezra took care of his aunt after his father's death. Then, one horrible afternoon, he had found Mary floating facedown in the pond behind the small cabin they had moved to. She had drowned herself.

Now I am alone, Ezra thought, after burying Mary beneath her favorite beech tree.

Thanks to William Goode, I am alone in the world.

The Goodes cursed my family.

The Goodes ruined our lives.

And now it is up to me to pay them back.

But where to begin? Where can I find out if any Goodes remain in the Colonies?

Ezra needed information to start his angry quest for revenge. Strapping his few possessions on his back and abandoning the small cabin in the woods, he returned now to Matthew's farm.

As the farmhouse came into view, Ezra urged the exhausted horse on, kicking its sides, whipping its neck with the worn leather reins.

I remember it, he thought, gazing at the two-story house in wonder and surprise. I remember that toolhouse at the edge of the garden. And that little house on the far side of the pasture—that was *my* house!

His heart pounded with excitement.

Are Matthew and Constance still here? he wondered.

As he rode closer, his excitement faded to disappointment. The pasture was high with overgrown weeds. There were no cows or sheep in sight. No crops. No bales of wheat or straw. The garden was barren and weed choked. Brambles and weeds stretched across the unplowed field.

The farm hadn't been worked in years, Ezra could see.

Did Matthew and Constance die? Did they abandon the farm after Father, Aunt Mary, and I left?

Eager to solve the mystery, eager to gain the information he needed to begin his quest for revenge against the Goodes, Ezra jumped down from the horse.

His legs ached from the long ride as he made his way to the front door. He took a deep breath. And knocked.

Silence.

The whisper of the wind through the shimmering trees was the only reply.

He knocked again. "Is anyone home?" His deep voice echoed strangely in the empty yard.

Ezra pushed open the door. Stepping inside, he found the front room dark and cold, despite the warmth of the afternoon. A layer of dust had settled over the furniture, making everything appear ghostly and unreal.

"Anyone home?" Ezra called loudly.

The floorboards creaked under his boots.

This room hasn't been used in years, he realized, rubbing his hand over a table, making a long smear in the covering of dust.

He had come so far, driven the horse so hard. He had been so eager to find his great-uncle, to speak to him, to hear the story of the Goodes, to learn where he could seek his revenge.

He had come so far to find only dust and silence.

"No!" Ezra cried. "I will find what I need in this dark old house!"

He began a rapid, determined search of all the rooms. The dining room was as gloomy and dust covered as the sitting room. In the common room two field mice gazed at him from the barren hearth, as if he were intruding in their domain.

Retracing his steps, Ezra moved quickly back toward Matthew's study, his features set in a disappointed frown.

Perhaps Matthew left some papers, Ezra thought hopefully. A journal or diary. Something that will tell me what I need to know.

The wooden door had become warped.

Ezra struggled to pull it open. It wouldn't budge.

"I cannot give up!" he cried. "I must see what lies behind this door!"

He sucked in a deep breath, grabbed the edge of the door, and pulled. With a burst of strength he finally managed to slide it open partway.

Breathing hard, he peered inside—and gasped.

Chapter
24

Ezra stared in amazement. At first he didn't believe his eyes.

The opening was covered by a wall of stone!

Ezra pulled the study door open a little farther.

"What on earth!" he exclaimed, scratching his dark hair. The room had been completely walled in.

Gaping in astonishment in the dim light, Ezra saw that the stones had been piled one on top of another but not cemented together.

"What I am looking for must certainly be on the other side of this strange wall," he said. The sound of his voice reassured him.

He reached for a stone and attempted to pull it away.

It was then that he heard the scratching sound.

He lowered his hands.

The scratching continued, low and steady.

Scratch, scratch, scratch.

More field mice? Ezra wondered, listening hard.

No. The sound is too regular, too steady.

Scratch, scratch, scratch.

What is making that sound?

With renewed energy Ezra began pulling the heavy stones out of the wall and tossing them down on the floor behind him.

Dust flew as he worked, choking him, burning his eyes.

The scratching sound grew louder.

Did my great-uncle wall in his own study? Ezra wondered as he worked, pulling the stones away, heaving them behind him.

Did he hide something in here that he didn't want anyone to find?

He could see only darkness through the small opening he had made. With a quiet groan he pulled away more stones.

He worked feverishly for several minutes, thinking about what he might find on the other side, pulling away stone after stone.

"So much dust," he muttered. "So many stones. . . ."

Blinking, he resumed his back-breaking work—and gasped.

A grinning decayed brown skull leaned toward him from the darkness on the other side of the wall.

Ezra tried to cry out—but he was too late.

The skull slid toward him.

The skeleton's brittle arm slid out through the hole in the wall, and its bony fingers closed around Ezra's throat!

Chapter
25

Ezra shrieked and fell backward, stumbling over the stones strewn at his feet.

He landed hard on his back. Stunned, he lay there for a moment, panting and staring up at the hole in the wall.

The skeleton arm was draped over the wall, not moving.

Still breathing hard, his back aching from his fall, Ezra climbed to his feet.

He peered into the opening he had made. The skeleton had merely fallen forward, he realized. It hadn't really grabbed him. But what was that scratching sound? Had the skeleton been trying to break free?

Ezra pushed the skeleton out of his way, raised himself up on his hands, and peered into the room. Too dark in there to see anything.

Grumbling, he turned back into the room, his eyes searching the grayness until he found a candle on a low table. Carrying the candle into the kitchen, he located a tinderbox near the hearth.

It took several minutes of concentrated work, rubbing the kindling together in a hard, fast rhythm, to get a small fire started. Then Ezra was able to light the candle. It flared, then flickered out, then flared again.

Eagerly he returned to the dark walled-in room.

A second skeleton greeted him on his return. This skeleton was seated at a low worktable.

Ezra held the candle close to the grinning skull. From all the decay he couldn't even tell which skeleton was his great-uncle Matthew and which was his great-aunt Constance.

In the yellow candle glow Ezra's eyes came to rest on a document on the table under the skeleton's bony hand. Pushing away the hand, Ezra carefully lifted the brittle papers.

Raising the candle close, he struggled to read the scrawled words on the page. "It's a journal!" he cried. "Written by Matthew Fier."

Eagerly Ezra read the words on the last page of the journal:

I still laugh the hideous laugh without cease, the laughter an unending torture for me and for Constance. But the wall is in place, and at last we are safe from the Goodes and their treachery.

Constance attempted to escape. The poor woman did not realize that the wall is for our safety. I had to hit her over the head and render her senseless so that I could put in place the final stones and secure our safety.

We are now as safe as we were in the old days in Wickham, and will remain safe from the Goodes for the rest of our lives.

The manuscript ended there.

Ezra set it down gently.

The Goodes, he thought.

The Goodes have destroyed my family. I will not rest until I find them. The Goodes must pay for their evil.

His heart pounding, Ezra took a step back.

The skeleton seated at the table suddenly creaked and toppled backward. In the dim light Ezra spied a strange object at its neck.

Holding the candle in front of him, Ezra leaned over the skeleton and lifted a round silver amulet from around the neck bone. He stared at the tiny three-toed claw in the center of the disk. Words were inscribed on the back of the medallion, but Ezra could not make them out in the dim light.

With a wistful sigh Ezra slipped the cord around his neck and adjusted the amulet over his chest. "My only inheritance," he said bitterly.

A few moments later he was out of the cold, dark house, walking into the sunshine, thinking about the village of Wickham, thinking about the Goodes, driven by his bitterness toward the sweetness of revenge.

Village of Shadyside
1900

Nora Goode hunched over her writing paper, the candlelight flickering over the small desk. She lowered her pen and took a moment to stretch her aching fingers.

"So much to tell," she said, staring into the yellow flame. "So much to write. This poor hand *must* hold out until my story is through."

And the story was just beginning, Nora knew.

The Fiers would continue to pay dearly for their betrayal of the Goodes. Blood would flow. The blood of both families, through decades.

"Yes, my frightening story has just begun," Nora whispered. "It is a long and bitter tale, and I must finish it before the night is over."

Bending to her task, she picked up the pen, dipped it into the inkwell, and feverishly began to write again.

TO BE CONTINUED . . .

About the Author

"Where do you get your ideas?" That's the question that R. L. Stine is asked most often.

"I don't know where my ideas come from," he says. "But I do know that I have a lot more scary stories in my mind that I can't wait to write."

So far, R.L. has written nearly three dozen mysteries and thrillers for young people, all of them bestsellers.

R.L. grew up in Columbus, Ohio. Today he lives in an apartment near Central Park in New York City with his wife, Jane, and thirteen-year-old son, Matt.

THE NIGHTMARES
NEVER END . . .
WHEN YOU VISIT

Next . . .
THE FEAR STREET SAGA:
THE SECRET

The bloody feud continues. Jonathan Fier wants
to marry a girl who could end the curse forever.
But Jonathan knows she's hiding something. Is
she telling the truth? Then two Fier sisters fall in
love with the same man—a man named Goode
—and their rivalry ends in death!

FEAR STREET®

R.L. Stine

R·L·STINE

presents

THE FEAR STREET®
1996 CALENDAR

Spend 1996 on
FEAR STREET

Vampires, evil cheerleaders, ghosts, and all the
boys and ghouls of R. L. Stine's Fear Street books
are here to help you shriek through the seasons.
It's the perfect way to keep track of your days,
nights, and nightmares....

Special Bonus Poster

A map of Shadyside showing where all the
horrors of Fear Street happened. Take a
terrifying tour of the spots where your favorite
characters lived—and died.

A Fear Street Calendar/Published by Archway Paperbacks

1098-M-01